ALEX ARCHER

— Town Secrets —

BRIAN SIMPSON

Fulton Books
Meadville, PA

Published by Fulton Books 2022

ISBN 978-1-63985-298-7 (paperback)
ISBN 978-1-63985-299-4 (digital)

Printed in the United States of America

AUTHOR'S NOTE

To my dearly departed wife, Rahsha, thank you for always believing in me and sticking with me through the toughest of times. You were an amazing wife and a mother who is sorely missed. Thank you to my sons, Jordan and Jalen, for being great sons and movie partners on the weekends. To my parents, Donald and Judith Simpson, thank you for being the types of parents who taught me to dream big and that I could accomplish anything that I put my mind to. My baby sister, Crystal, for always considering me her hero regardless of any mistakes that I may have made. My grandparents, Robert and Georgia Mack and Tessie Simpson, for always reminding me to keep the Lord first. Thanks to Robin Clarke for helping me clean things up. Thanks to Technical Sergeant David Anding for fact-checking and accuracy. Lastly, to my fourth-grade classmate, Ha Tran, for telling me that she enjoyed listening to my stories that I wrote in Mrs. Etherton's class at Edgewater Elementary School in Pensacola, Florida. You may not remember me, but I remember sitting next to you in class back then and telling me that I would be a writer when I grew up. I guess you were right. Good call!

CHAPTER 1

As the saying goes, "There's no place like home." I don't know exactly who said that, but I can only guess that they're referring to that feeling that you get when you think about home: the nostalgia that one experiences when they think about growing up in their hometown. Memories of summer barbecues, first days of school, family, friends, and more, all help to make up that warm and fuzzy feeling you get in your stomach when you think about going home. Maybe that's why a guy like me is making this long drive home. Despite growing up on the poor east side of the tracks, my hometown of Patrician seems to be calling my name. I left after high school. Didn't see much reason to stay back then. Wasn't a lot going on in the east side of Patrician at the time, so I took the first track scholarship that I was offered. I left with no intentions of ever returning except to visit my parents during the holidays or maybe on an occasional random weekend visit.

I didn't like the division in Patrician. The natural divide in a city separated by railroad tracks and race never set right with me, so I took off out of there as soon as the opportunity presented itself. As a kid, I loved the occasional visits we would make to the west side of town. Crossing the tracks felt like going to an entirely different world. People wore nice clothes, drove nice cars which they pulled up to nice houses. The plazas, tall buildings, and beaches all made me feel like the west side of Patrician was where I wanted to be. That feeling always seemed to get stamped out rather quickly when my family and I spent what people on that side of town viewed as a little too much time in one of those plazas, tall buildings, or on one of the beaches. It didn't matter how much I felt like I belonged on that side of town; west side Patricianites had a way of letting you know that you didn't belong there.

My parents would notice the stares and sneers that we got for being Black people who dared cross the tracks. My dad in particular made sure to tell me that I had every right to go to that side of town as anyone who actually lived there. Regardless of what Dad said, I was usually ready to go after I saw one too many of those looks directed at me or my family. It wasn't just the sneers and looks of disgust that cast a cloud on my ventures to the west side; it was this feeling of uneasiness I always got after being there. Sure, I knew that we were unwelcomed by many who lived there, and that fact alone generated stares, but the uneasiness I'm talking about is the type of uneasiness that comes when you know you're being watched—kinda like what I would imagine a gazelle would feel if it were walking in a field on an African plain, and everything suddenly became eerily quiet and still. I would sometimes feel the same on the east side as well, but there I couldn't figure out why. No one on the east side hated me being there, so I remember being puzzled when that feeling of being watched came over me.

I do remember not being the only one who felt this uneasiness about Patrician. I recall once hearing my mother say that living in East Patrician felt like knowing someone was keeping a secret about you, but you didn't know what the secret was, or even who was keeping it. I have often thought about her saying that, even more so now that I am going home, but I could never quite figure out what she meant. Maybe she was just talking about the overall tension in the air that came from living in a city separated by so many things in both a literal and figurative sense. Maybe she was talking about how things seemed to work out well on the west side of Patrician and not so well on the east. Regardless, it spooked the hell outta me, and I knew that I wanted to get away from that sense of dread and uneasiness I would get even if it was not a regular occurrence for me.

I suppose it'll be good to be home. There is a lot I missed while I was away. After I realized that the Olympic Games weren't a reality for me, I was faced with a choice: go back to Patrician and be another in a long line of has-been athletes who left only to return with their tail between their legs or take Uncle Sam's offer to see the world while serving my country. I love my country but never saw myself as the soldier type. I also never saw myself going back to Patrician, so the moment I had my degree in hand, off I went into the wild blue yonder! At first, I thought I'd go in, give Uncle Sam a couple of years, and then find something else to do. One reenlistment turned to six, and before I knew it, I had become a career man. Twenty whole years in the Air Force, and I loved every minute of it. I can be a bit of an adrenalin junkie, so I was looking for adventure when I joined; but I, like many, have an aversion to taking a bullet, so I chose something that didn't require me to risk getting shot. My adrenal drug of choice was the KC-135 Stratotanker. Nothing got me more excited than getting up in the air in that monster! I suppose the sound of the engines, the power you feel going down the runway, the excitement of leaving the ground and having another jet fly up to you and connect midair were enough to keep me hooked for twenty years. But now it's all over, and I have to find something else to get into.

I'm kinda curious about what I will find in Patrician now that so much time has passed. It's been at least fifteen years since I've seen the place. Mom and Dad were always looking for a reason to travel, so they made it a point to come and visit me wherever I was stationed. Before I knew it, a lot of years had passed since I had been back. When I left, Patrician was this superficial kind of place. People, especially those on the west side, were all into image. Who's dating who? Who's driving what? What kind of job do you have? Blah, blah, blah. You didn't need substance or character to make it there. You just needed to have the right look and the right money. With those, a person could have anything they needed. With that combination, the city could become intoxicating. The bright lights and big city mixed with beach life lulled many a Patricianite to the type of social sleep they couldn't wake up from. I have seen good moral agents like preachers or kindergarten teachers move in, take one whiff of that Patrician air, and become so morally mixed up they would step over a guy with a legitimate hard-luck story in order to feed a stray dog. Such a beautiful city to look at with all its architectural splendor, but even all that coastal and urban beauty could never hide the fact that something was seriously wrong with Patrician. You couldn't clearly see it, but you could damn sure feel it. You could feel it on the corner. You could feel it at the park. You could feel it at school. You may not have been able to put your finger on it, but something was definitely going on.

Despite my misgivings about going home, I was excited about seeing some of the friends I left behind when I went away. I had some friends I was really close to, mostly neighborhood kids that I grew up with and teammates. I had a lot of love for them, and for a split second, I almost changed my mind about leaving because of them. Glad my common sense prevailed because many of them decided to leave too. Those who did leave just came back quicker than I did. Kinda makes me wonder if coming back was part of a grand scheme that God had for me and those others who left only to return. Not trying to think bigger of myself than I should, but maybe a bunch of fresh perspectives from people who know the city can help it to change for the better. Maybe get that damned eeriness out of the air. Ah…who am I kidding? I'm going back home to lay low and chill. I'm not old, but I've been around the block enough times to want to stop going around it for a bit. Time to go home, see family, say hello to friends and a few coaches, and begin to enjoy this retirement—this working retirement. A low-stress something or other to supplement and evenings on the beach sounded like a plan to me.

There are very few things as simultaneously calming and exhilarating as driving into a beach city on a summer day. I always enjoyed when Dad would take my sister, Devin, and me to the beach. My cousins Nikki, Robert, and Allen lived on the same street, and they always seemed to have a sixth sense for when Daddy was taking us to the beach. It never failed; we would start getting ready to go to the beach, and the three of them would knock on the door in succession: Nikki first because she lived next door, followed by Allen and Robert who lived across the street and around the corner. If I really want to be truthful about it, my cousins' collective sixth sense about Daddy taking us to the beach was probably enhanced by my telling them when he planned to take us. "How in the world do they always show up when we're getting ready to go to the beach?" he would ask while looking at Devin and me. She and I would just look at each other, seemingly perplexed about why he thought we would know. Devin would always explain how coincidental it was while I slipped off to the bathroom to avoid being asked. Like clockwork...*knock, knock, knock!* Daddy would walk to the door in his beach clothes while looking at Devin who was standing there, looking as cluelessly innocent as possible.

"Hey, Uncle Dave! You taking Alex and Devin to the beach today?" Nikki would ask.

"Not sure yet, baby girl. You need to talk to Devin!"

Nikki would always nod and follow Devin to the den. I would emerge from the bathroom and go to the kitchen. *Knock, knock, knock!*

"Lemme guess," Dad would say as he opened the door to find Allen and Robert standing there.

They'd storm in while calling, "Hey, Uncle Dave!" and rush to the kitchen to see me.

Nikki would always try to not make it too obvious that we were all scheming to go to the beach together—Robert and Allen not so much. After a few weeks into the summer, these two nuts would just show up to the door, wearing swimming trunks and holding beach towels. Allen even showed up with his dog a few times, to which Dad would always respond with a perplexed frown that signaled to Allen that he needed to take his dog back home very quickly to avoid being left behind. After two summers of this, Dad didn't even fight anymore. He'd just open the door and let them in. It got so bad after a while he sold his Trans-Am and bought a pickup so he could haul us all to the beach in the back of it. I loved the Trans-Am and hated to see it go, but I loved what the truck could do even more. The Trans-Am meant looking cool, riding around with Dad and having the top off so people could see how cool I looked in it. The truck meant that Dad couldn't tell Devin and me there wasn't enough room to take Nikki, Robert, and Allen to the beach with us anymore. Of course, the truck didn't look as good as the Trans-Am, but it was cool for a truck: a huge red-and-white Ford F-150. We nick-named it Big Red. Seeing my sister and cousins jump in the back of Big Red made me quickly get over not looking cool in the Trans-Am anymore.

After a quick stop at the corner store, we would head directly to the beach. Big Red wouldn't come to a complete stop before the five of us hopped out of the back, and it was a race to the water. Allen always lost the race because in mid-sprint he would always feel the need to turn around and ask my mom, "Aunt Jamie, you brought food, right?" She always smiled and responded, "Go play, Allen," while helping Dad with the cooler that was packed with sandwiches she made the night before and bringing the chips that Dad had just purchased at the corner store. I guess he was always so caught up into the fun of the ride and conversation he never paid attention to what was happening right in front of him. We used to give him a lot of lip about that because something could be going on right in front of him, and he'd completely miss it. That almost got him in serious trouble once.

Beach and port cities like Patrician can attract a lot of strange passersby. Allen, being the oblivious type of kid he was, ran into one of these weirdos at the beach once. When we were about twelve years old, Allen, Robert, and I were playing frisbee on the beach. One of our favorite challenges playing frisbee was to have the disc thrown in your direction and over your head so you would have to run after it to catch it before it hit the ground. If you caught it, you were considered fast; if not, you were picked on for being too slow. Serves to me very rarely hit the ground. It actually became a challenge for my sister and cousins to see if they could throw the frisbee hard and fast enough for me to miss it. Robert caught it half the time. Devin was a lost cause. She's my sister, but God must have skipped over her when he was handing out speed because she was as slow as a sloth with an injured leg. Nikki caught the disc most of the time, like me, but she was the type of girl who worried about sweating her hair out of place; so after catching about four or five, she would go hang out with Devin to avoid sweating. That left Allen. Now, truth be told, Allen was about as fast as I was. On any given day, he would push me to whatever finish line we had established before we raced, or even nip me at the line. When that happened, I would either call a tie or say that he started too early. The only real difference in our running was that Allen wasn't very coordinated. He was fine running in a straight line, but if you asked him to turn left or right, he was almost certain to have a fall that looked like it should be in an action movie. Like normal, I threw the frisbee hard and fast so Allen would have to chase it down. I threw it slightly right away from the water so he would have difficulty catching up to it. Now Allen had had some serious falls in the past, but this one was *epic*. This was professional stuntman level! The wind caught the frisbee and carried it toward a sand dune. When Allen and the sand dune met, the sand dune won. The only thing missing from this fall was a Hollywood blockbuster-style explosion. Even more epic than his collision with the sand dune was the laughter that ensued. It got even louder when Allen emerged covered from head to toe in sand. My cousins and I were always quick to laugh; Dad was too. Mom was the one who tried to hold back a laugh if it were at someone's expense, so Allen knew that he must have had a good one when he stood up and saw my mother with her hand over her mouth and her shoulders bouncing up and down, trying to conceal her laughter. Allen was always a good sport about it because he knew how clumsy he could be. Most of

the time, he just laughed with us. This time was no different…except for I got that eerie feeling again.

Despite the hilarity, out of nowhere, that weird feeling
draped over me like a cold, wet blanket on a winter day. We
finally stopped laughing, and Allen decided he needed to
get the sand off himself, so he started walking toward the
beach showers that were stationed so a person could rinse
off before leaving.

"Where you going, Allen?"

"To rinse off this sand."

"Just jump in the water!"

"I have sand in my eye. I'll be right back."

The shower was maybe a hundred yards away from
where Dad parked Big Red on the beach—close enough
to see it, but far enough away to feel the distance. Keeping
my eye on Allen was my focus because I had a sense that
something just wasn't quite right. Just as Allen turned on
the shower, I saw Devin walk by with a strawberry soda.
Strawberry was the flavor I always asked Dad to pick for
me. Devin, being the annoying little sister that she was
back then, knew that drinking my sodas would irritate
the hell out of me; walking in front of me while doing so
just sent me over the edge. I stormed off in her direction,
intent on snatching my strawberry soda from her when I
noticed over her shoulder that the shower Allen was using
to rinse off was now empty. Allen was nowhere in sight. I
took off toward the shower as fast as I could and passed the
retention wall stairs that led to the parking lot hoping to
see Allen near the concession booth—nothing. Out of the
corner of my eye, I saw a Ford F-150 just like Big Red, only

painted black, and walking toward it was Allen. About four paces in front of him were a man and a woman. The man was nothing special to look at: kind of pale, average height, blondish-brown hair, not in bad shape, but by no means the type of physique that would turn heads. The woman was another story: silky black hair down to the middle of her back, light olive-colored skin, and a body like a fitness instructor. It was almost as if Wonder Woman was walking in front of me. A rush of emotions and thoughts filled the pit of my stomach and my head.

In a split-second, thoughts like, *Who are these people?* and *Why is Allen following them?* and *He shouldn't be with them. This is bad,* all bounced around in my head before instinct took over, and I blurted out, "Allen...it's time to eat!"

Like a person being snapped out of a hypnotic trance, Allen turned around like nothing was wrong and said, "What's up, Alex?" while the man and woman kept walking toward their truck without turning around.

Allen jogged back toward me while telling me about this man and woman he had just met who were parked across the street. Other than hearing him say something about a dog and a truck, I can't remember a word of what Allen said because by this time, I had become somewhat fixated on these people who had captured Allen's attention. They got to their truck and said a few words to each other while the woman walked to the passenger side, and they got into the truck.

The man turned toward us and asked, "Do you still want to see it?"

Allen grabbed me by the wrist and said, "Let's go see their dog!"

"Allen!" I said in a low but sharp voice. "Are you stupid or something? Why are you walking to these people's car? We don't even know them!"

A sudden look of realization mixed with confusion and fear came over Allen's face.

"He's right here, Allen," the man said as both of us stood there, definitely scared.

To make things even weirder, we noticed the street was eerily still and quiet despite it being the middle of the day near a crowded beach.

"No, thank you, sir," Allen said as I grabbed his wrist while backtracking toward the beach. "He's right here, fellas. Won't take you long at all to look at him."

"We're good!"

"You came up here to see the dog, Allen," he said while walking toward us.

"I said we're good, man!" I reiterated as Allen and I started to jog away.

Just as we reached the retention wall stairs, we saw Devin and Nikki approaching.

"Where'd y'all go?" Nikki asked, followed immediately by Devin asking, "What's up with you two?"

I spread out my arms to block and corral the three of them so I could usher them back toward Dad, Mom, and Robert. They all turned around, and Allen began to nervously stammer through his description of what happened. As I grabbed the stair rail to go back down the steps, I turned around expecting to see the man across the street getting into his truck to leave. Instead, he was standing there in front of the truck with his hands in his pockets and his gaze fixated on me.

A few awkward seconds passed, and the man gave me this sly smile and said, "See ya around, kid."

To say a chill went down my spine that moment is an understatement. It felt more like the blood in my veins had turned to ice water. Hearing Nikki say, "Alex, let's go," helped to loosen the chokehold of fear clutching my neck and allowed me to turn and go down the retention wall stairs. Dad could tell by the way that we ran over to him and Mom that something wasn't right. It took only a few moments to explain to him what had happened and return to the stairs, but by the time we got there, the man, the woman, and the truck were gone—vanished like steam in a gentle breeze. From that day forward, we as kids were changed. It wasn't like we lost innocence or anything. We just came to realize that the scary people your parents and teachers tell you about will sometimes rear their heads to let you know that they're around.

CHAPTER 2

Going Home

Nothing helps to clear your head like a long drive by your-self; one of the longest drives in America has to be from Spokane, Washington, to Patrician, Florida. Crossing the country in a plane can sometimes make you forget how beautiful America is at ground level, so I decided last month that I would drive back to Patrician instead of fly. I headed to Spokane to pick up my rental car as soon as I dropped my papers at Fairchild AFB. A guy like me gets to know a lot of people when you spend as many years on one base as I have. After duty assignments at McConnell AFB and Seymour Johnson AFB, I landed at Fairchild. Wasn't too excited about going there at first, but when you have no choice in the matter, you make it work. I went there with an open mind, and it ended up being a great experience. Made a lot of friends with people on the base as well as in Spokane, so there was no way I was going to hit the road without seeing a few friends before I left.

After I dropped my papers off, Lieutenant Michele Paulson was waiting out front to take me to the rental car office in her new GMC Sierra. It was new to her, but not to me. I sold it to her the moment I announced I was going to retire. She loved the truck and had been bugging me about buying it from my first mention of selling it when I retired.

After a few steps out of the office, I heard, "Hurry up, Archer! A sista is starving over here. You sure you were a track star? 'Cause you walk slow as hell."

As I walked to the truck, shaking my head and rolling my eyes, I couldn't help but think about how much I was going to miss her smart mouth.

With a laugh, I said, "Shut up and drive," and climbed in the truck. My butt wasn't fully in the seat before she was pulling off.

We drove to the rental car office where I picked up a Camaro, and then we headed straight to Benny's Bar and Grill. Lots of good times and a lot of money spent in Benny's. Not much to look at, but there was no place Paulson and I would rather stop to get something to eat after a training exercise. Lt. Paulson was my copilot on the KC-135s and we flew many missions together. Through thick and thin, Michelle Paulson has been right there. Met her the first day I arrived at McConnell twenty years ago and except for one time in our careers, we always somehow ended up at the same duty stations. That type of friendship in the military has really helped over the years.

I thought we were only meeting a few friends from our hangar, but when I walked through the door, it felt like "Alex Archer Day." My entire crew showed up. I was especially happy to see Staff Sgt. Patrick Walls when I walked in. Dark-skinned kid, about twenty-nine years old, six feet two inches, and a chiseled 220 pounds, he looked like he was carved out of a block of obsidian; always smiling and always something positive to say. As my boom operator, Walls always provided a much-needed balance to all the sarcasm between Michelle and me on the plane.

"Sure gonna miss you, Major! At least now I have a place to stay when I want to go to Florida!" he said with his signature smile.

"As long as I'm in Patrician, you have a vacation spot."

"What about me?" chimed in Michelle.

"You'll have to wait until I get my shed built in the backyard."

"Okay… I had that one coming, Arch. But seriously, you better get a place big enough for me to stay when I decide to grace Patrician with my presence."

About six or seven insults raced across my mind when she said that, and judging by how fast she said, "Leave it there, Archer!" my face gave it away.

The night went on with food, drinks, sarcasm, and stories, all of which helped me remember how good those past ten years had been at Fairchild. I'm not an overly emotional type of guy, but seeing all the smiles and listening to people I had gotten to know pretty well over the years really did my heart some good. Leaving is hard, but I knew deep down that home was tugging on my heart for a reason. After all the hugs and goodbyes, I followed Michelle back to her house where we reminisced and laughed a bit more before I crashed on her couch for the night.

The next day I woke up at zero dark thirty. I'm not much of a drinker, so I didn't have any hangover blues to deal with. I told Michelle that I would probably just sneak out without waking her and call her from the road when the day got underway. I did the normal morning thing in her guest bathroom: brushed my teeth, showered, washed my face, and came out ready to go, only to see Michelle standing in the doorway of her bedroom.

"You didn't have to get up, Michelle. I was going to call you from the road."

"I know, but how can someone sleep with you stomping around like a herd of bison? Besides, you really didn't think I was gonna let you leave without at least saying 'I'll see your big head later,' did you?" she asked.

"You're gonna really miss me, aren't you, Michelle?"

"A little bit. Who else am I gonna talk noise to at Benny's? But I really won't have time to miss you too much anyway."

"Why's that?"

"My father just retired from McDonnell Douglass, and he just bought Mom the house that she always wanted in Ft. Myers. They haven't liked me being so far away from them, so they've already been laying the guilt trip on me about moving closer to them when they get there. I've been trying to avoid that topic when they bring it up, but now that my boy Archer is going back to Florida, the idea doesn't sound too bad anymore. Patrician's not too far away, so it doesn't look like you're gonna be rid of me yet when I transfer to MacDill in three months. And you can keep your funky little shed in your backyard too."

"Great…just when I thought I was going to have a break from your smart-ass mouth for a while."

"Oh, whatever! Get on the road and drive safely, Lead Foot. Call and let me know when you stop for the night."

And with that, I gave Michelle a hug, jumped in the Camaro, dropped the top, and hit the road. Just me, my thoughts, my playlist, and the open road. I was looking forward to seeing if what they said about the cops in Montana and South Dakota not caring if a person speeds was true.

Along with time alone to think, another great thing about driving cross-country is the opportunity to see interesting things and meet different people. I've flown over things like Mt. Rushmore countless times in the past, but I've never actually stopped to look at them. It felt good to not have a deadline, so I figured stopping to take in some sights right now would do me some good. I had a lot to think about in terms of what to do next. I'd spent the last twenty years giving orders (based on the orders that I had been given), so the idea of not having to order around or take orders from anyone felt a bit strange. Like always, I'd figure it out. I just needed to make sure that it didn't take too long for me to figure it out.

Mom and Devin said that Patrician has changed. Some for the better, some for the worse. Dad couldn't care less either way. He just wants to watch sports and fish in the evenings; so as long as he has those, he's a happy man. With all the work he put in over the past thirty-five years, the old man has earned that right. I was definitely looking forward to seeing him fire up the grill on Saturday afternoons, or any afternoon for that matter. Definitely needed to make sure that I contacted Allen, Robert, and Nikki as soon as I got back too. We hadn't physically seen each other in years, but I was glad that we'd all stayed close. Besides, they would hang me upside down if I came back in town and didn't stop by within hours of arriving. I knew I'd be tired when I pulled in, but I already know that I'd find the energy to go see them. They were all married now and had young kids, so I had a couple of nieces, nephews, and cousins that wanted to meet Uncle/Cousin Alex.

It was going to be interesting to see the changes that Mom and Devin were talking about. Hopefully, the changes didn't only benefit the west side of Patrician. It would be rather refreshing to see that something good finally came to the east side so everyone could benefit. The last good thing I remember coming to the east side was a little clinic for people who couldn't afford health care. That was cool, but a community can't thrive with just a clinic. The east side needed banks, grocery stores, police departments, and other necessities in order to thrive. I remember Dad talking about how city government always seemed to ignore the needs of the east side. It really did my heart a lot of good to hear that Devin, Allen, Nikki, and Robert led the charge to get the former mayor out of office.

Mayor Stuart catered primarily to the needs of the west side and only ventured into the east side during an election year; the type of guy who on a normal day wouldn't be caught dead on the east side but somehow managed to find his way to an African Methodist Episcopal Church service and a fish fry when it was time to campaign. He wasn't too happy when he got voted out, and he really wasn't too happy to know how it happened. A lot of people I know voted out of civic duty. They didn't know the candidates very well and knew even less about what they stood for, so ended up voting for a familiar name and face. Old Man Stuart won that way for years. He simply showed his face, made a few promises in an east-side church or two that he rarely kept, and he got enough of the east-side vote to stay in office. It was a good cycle for him, but a bad cycle for us. Promises for more funding and police to stop the rising crime on the east side were never kept, but east siders either kept voting for him or didn't vote at all. Knowing that he got voted out because a few people he used to lie to and ignore helped to steer votes away from him didn't sit too well. He suffered a massive stroke about three months after his defeat. I certainly don't celebrate the demise of another human being, but I was glad that to know that the same old dirty politics might not be going on anymore. Robert told me that Devin did a lot of the legwork to sway voters away from Old Man Stuart. She was knocking on doors, visiting churches, making fliers, and anything else she could think of to get the word about the need for change on the east side of Patrician. Hopefully, the new mayor had a heart for the city as a whole and not just for the west side.

A fast car and the open road can be calming for a guy like me. The rental car company didn't have a Camaro SS in stock, so they transferred one in for me from one of their stores in Seattle. It took them about a week to get it, but the manager said he was more than happy to bring it in for me. He was retired Air Force as well and said he wanted to do what he could to make sure I went out in style. His nametag read "Charles," an older guy who appeared to be in his mid-sixties, the type of guy with a friendly demeanor and eyes suggesting he had an interesting story. I had a lot fun trading Air Force stories with him the day I came in to see if they could bring in a Camaro. When he told me he could find me a Camaro SS, I asked, "Well, how about a ZL1?"

"Don't push it, son. Ol' Chuck had to pull this SS out of Seattle. You'll have me going all the way down to San Francisco for one of those," he responded with a laugh.

"Just figured I'd ask. I didn't expect you to have the SS available."

"A guy driving one of these to Florida sounds like he wants to open it up on the road in Montana or the Dakotas. Be careful with that," he said with a wink and a smile as I shook his hand.

"You're all right, Chuck. I'll stop by and say hello when I come back to visit."

I probably should have listened to Chuck when he told me to be careful with opening up this SS in the Dakotas because I got stopped twice in South Dakota! The first guy let me off with a warning near the North Dakota / South Dakota state line, but a second one got me about halfway through. He probably radioed ahead and told his partner to be on the lookout for some nut in a Camaro SS who heard he could drive through South Dakota like a Formula One racer.

When I stopped in Kansas City for some barbecue, I decided to take a detour through Tulsa, Oklahoma. Had a few college friends that lived there. They got into real estate and the oil and gas industries and did pretty well, so dinner and lodging were on them.

After leaving Tulsa, I decided to take my time the rest of the way. I was so focused on how fast I could burn through Montana and the Dakotas I forgot to look at the beauty of the countryside. My friends in Tulsa posted pics on social media about the fun we had while I was there. A few high school and college friends who had relocated to Dallas told me they would hunt me down like a dog if I was that close to them and didn't stop through on the way home. Those pics also got me in hot water with my friends who relocated to Southern California. They were heated that I left the northwest without going there first. That meant a trip to California was on the horizon; I would never live it down if I didn't make it.

After two days in Dallas and more pics on social media, I got calls from friends in New Orleans, Atlanta, Raleigh, Washington, D.C., Jacksonville, and New Smyrna Beach, Florida—in all of which I stopped and spent a day or two. A trip that was originally supposed to take three days wound up taking three weeks. Some of those friends and I hadn't seen each other in over a decade, so it was great reconnecting and seeing how much we had all accomplished in the past ten to twenty years or so. That was time and money well spent. Being in the military makes one conscious of time and deadlines, so I naturally had put myself on a schedule to get to Patrician. Thank God for lifelong friends who helped me to stop and smell the proverbial roses on my way home. Thank God for unlimited miles on a rental car too because I put that to the test with this Camaro SS.

CHAPTER 3

Late April mornings in New Smyrna Beach are beautiful, so I couldn't leave the Atlantic side of Florida without catching one of its amazing sunrises. On a clear morning, the horizon casts the most glorious sienna shade you'll ever lay your eyes on. My mother would take me to see these sunrises when we would visit relatives who live here. After taking in the sunrise, I drove up to Ponce Inlet and climbed to the top of the lighthouse to take a few pictures then grabbed some food nearby. New Smyrna Beach has what I believe to be the best Dairy Queen in the world. It sits right off of US-1, so I figured I'd probably double back and get some ice cream after I got breakfast. There wasn't a cloud in the sky, so I could look to the south and see the assembly building at NASA. Growing up in a state where aviation and space exploration is such a mainstay, I guess I couldn't help falling in love with the idea of being a pilot.

Just as I was thinking about driving down to NASA to look around a little, I saw Devin's name pop up on my phone's caller ID.

"Lemme guess...you're either driving to NASA or at least thinking about doing it, huh?" Devin asked.

"Of course not. I'm on International Speedway Drive, getting ready to get on I-95 and connect to I-4."

"Okay, whatever, Alex. Get out of whatever you have climbed up on to look down the coastline at NASA and get your butt to Patrician. I can hear the people around you in the background. You know Momma and Daddy are worrying me to death, asking if you have left New Smyrna Beach yet. Daddy's been preparing food for the past three days. Get your butt on the road, man!"

"I have my window down at the stoplight, and the people you hear are walking across the crosswalk. Tell Mom and Dad that I'm driving now," I said while running down the lighthouse stairs.

I jumped in the Camaro, dropped the top, and peeled out. If I know my sister like I know I do, Devin called Mom and Dad and told them I had gone to visit NASA or something other than what I told her to say. She's two years younger than I, but I swear she thinks she's my other mother.

Once I hit I-4, it seemed like I blinked, and I was passing through Orlando. I blinked again, and I was in Tampa heading south toward Patrician. I guess after three weeks of being on the road, I was finally ready to get home and was also beginning to feel a sense of urgency about it. Not because I had a lot of family and friends who were waiting to see me; I just felt like there was something that I needed to see, as if I knew that someone had a secret to tell me, only I didn't have the slightest idea of who that could be and what they had to tell me. Aside from that, the only thing I could think about as I neared Patrician was Devin telling me that Dad was preparing food! A lot of guys think they can grill because they have the big smokers, but I'm not impressed. Give my dad a tripod grill and some mesquite chips, and he'll put anyone to shame.

With that in mind, I had a huge smile on my face as I hit the off-ramp at the end of the bridge that takes you into Patrician. Looked like they had done a lot of improvements near the ports. The bridges crossing the Patrician River that used to be drawbridges were now fixed and high enough for the ships to simply go under without stopping traffic on the bridge. The west side has always had all the bells and whistles that a city could ask for, but it was great to see that nicer things were finally starting to trickle into the east side as well. Seeing a Starbucks mingled in with the locally owned mainstay restaurants and shops spoke progress to me for some odd reason. Maybe it was all the time I'd spent up in Washington.

I grew up on Shelton Street in Patrician, and to this very day, I think it is the most beautiful street in the world. The American elms and southern magnolias on both sides of the street connect about thirty feet over the street, creating this beautifully captivating canopy. At the end of the canopy sits the house that I grew up in, which was still as warm and inviting as it had always been to me. Driving up and seeing Dad in the yard, Mom in the doorway, and the car parked in the driveway made me feel as if I had driven through a time warp for a split second. It didn't feel like I had never left; it just felt like I was home, like I belonged here despite any misgivings I had about Patrician in the past. Dad's smile lighting up his face while he stood by the grill and Mom stepping off the porch to meet me in the yard cemented those sentiments even more. I smiled, took a deep breath, and said to myself, "I'm home."

"Hey, boy!" has been my Dad's standard greeting for me since I can remember. It doesn't matter how old I get; I feel esteemed when I hear it. He wiped his hands on his apron, gave me a big hug, and said with a grin, "You were in that lighthouse looking at that NASA building when your sister called, weren't you?"

My mouth opened to prepare to give him one of the six answers I had prepared on the way from Ponce Inlet, but the only thing came out of my mouth behind a laugh was, "How'd you know?"

"I'm Dad... I know everything."

"Almost everything," chimed in Mom. "Knowing everything is my job. How was your drive, son? You went all over creation before getting here."

"Not over all creation, Momma. Maybe half of it."

Dad said, "Leave that boy alone, Jamie. I know he's your baby, but a man's gotta clear his head sometimes."

"No...get him, Aunt Jamie. He knows we've been waiting on him," said Allen. Now, we'd talked on the phone and over social media but it'd been years since I'd laid eyes on him. "Don't start, Alex," he said as he noticed me staring at his waistline.

"We're going to the gym tomorrow, cuz. The married life has been a little too good to you," I said as I patted him on his belly.

From behind me I heard, "Talk to him, cuz! I've been telling him that he's starting to get big!"

Robert shut the door of his Navigator, jogged up, and in one motion hugged me, picked me up, and ran across the front yard with me in his arms while laughing. Same old Robert: always upbeat, always smiling, with the type of laugh that makes you laugh when you hear it. He had a lot to smile and laugh about. A lot of people graduated high school and went off to college and started life elsewhere like I did. Robert did not. He came back to Patrician right after graduating from the University of South Florida with a degree in finance and became a banker. He married his college sweetheart, Jessica, and they started having kids almost immediately. Their two kids, Chris and Erika, were now in college and high school. Hard to believe how fast they grew up. Robert always had a head for numbers, so no one was surprised to see him become such a success in the banking world.

Nikki and her husband, Greg, pulled up next. I hadn't met their kids yet. For whatever reason, those two decided to wait until their thirties to have kids, and they were now in their late thirties with elementary school kids. The only thing their family planning seemed to accomplish is that they are the two oldest and most tired people at the PTA meetings. Robert and Jessica love to send pictures to them from cruises with the caption, "You wish you were here! Too bad your kids have to be at school tomorrow! LOL!" Nikki and Greg always returned the favor by staying out past the time they said they would return when Robert and Jessica would babysit for them. Devin's kids, Candace and Calvin, don't require babysitters anymore, so Devin and

Mike are ahead in their little game at this point. It's all in love though.

My loudmouthed sister finally pulled up. Devin is the type where you will hear her before you see her; never minces her words and is *never* afraid to tell you what she thinks even if you don't care to hear it.

"About time, Alex Archer!" she said. "You know your niece and nephew want to see you! You got Momma and Daddy worrying me to death, asking me about your every move. And I know you were in that lighthouse looking at the NASA building when I called. Where's Daddy? I gotta talk to him. Good to see you, bro," she said, seemingly in one breath, as she hugged me and walked toward Dad. He looked at her with a look of confusion and irritation.

"Man...how do you put up with that all day?" I asked my brother-in-law, Mike.

"I smile, say 'Okay, baby', and the day goes by smoothly."

"Well, I used to throw something at her when we were kids, and that worked for me. You should try it."

"You're trying to get me killed, Alex. You know that won't work for me, man," he said as we cracked up laughing.

As Mike and I caught up and laughed at Dad, we watched the patience begin to dissipate from his body as Devin talked to him about God knows what. I heard one of the sounds I had been waiting to hear since I dropped off my retirement papers and decided to move back to Patrician: "*Uncle Alex!*" two car doors slamming, footsteps rapidly moving in my direction. Before I could turn around fully, I was overwhelmed with hugs from two of my favorite people on earth, my niece, Candace, and her twin brother, Calvin. Candace is the spitting image of Devin, only not nearly as talkative. She looks like a runway model. Devin told me the boys at school are lined up, but Candace is into her books; despite being seventeen, she still thinks boys are annoying. If I had it my way, she'd stay that way until she was forty-five. I know that's not reality, but a guy can dream. Calvin is the complete opposite: spitting image of Mike, but talks like Devin. If a thought pops into his head, there's a 95 percent chance that it will somehow find its way out of his mouth. He is a bundle of personality and absolutely hilarious. They say that people most like you tend to annoy you, so it's no surprise that he gets under Devin's skin sometimes in a way that only a son can. Of course, Uncle Alex comes to the rescue when Devin has hit her limit with his mouth. It's not that he talks back. Mike and Devin don't play that at all. I just think he's the only person on the planet who can match Devin word for word, and I don't think that she has ever gotten used to that. My coming to Calvin's rescue when Devin has had her limit drives her up the wall, which is why I love doing it. I think getting under Devin's skin became a source of entertainment for Calvin and me when he and his sister were little. Whenever they came to visit me in Fairchild, or when I would come home to visit, I would always get Calvin talking. It didn't take much to start him up, and once he got going, he wasn't going to stop until either something caught his attention or he fell asleep. I'd come home for a few days on leave and take Candace and Calvin out for ice cream. About twenty minutes before taking them back to

Devin and Mike, I'd fill him up with a little more sugar and new information to talk about and then drop him back off with Devin. I'd carry them both up to the door in my arms, with Calvin chattering away, and say, "Here ya go!" with a huge sarcastic smile on my face. I could hear him talking away through the door as I walked back to my truck. Payback for years of talking my ears off when my friends or girlfriends would come over and any other way she chose to irritate me as only a little sister could.

"Hey, Uncle Alex! I'm glad you're back!" Candace said.

"What's up, Unk! Looking good, man! Mom says you're back for good now! I like that car too! Let's take it to get some ice cream. Can I drive it? What did you do with the truck from the pictures?" Calvin said in one breath.

I just laughed and said, "Slow down, man!" as I threw him the keys.

I don't think he expected me to say yes because the look on his face registered excitement and surprise at the same time.

Dad saw me from the corner of his eye during his conversation with Devin and asked, "Where you going, Alex?" with a hint of desperation in his voice.

I simply pointed to Calvin sitting in the front seat of the Camaro, who by this time was so excited about driving it he talked about its features and options even though no one else was yet in the car with him.

It was at this point that I watched Dad have a moment of reckoning. On one hand, he was in a conversation with Devin that he desperately wanted out of, but his only escape was to jump in a car with a child who likes to talk so much he is currently talking despite no one listening to him.

He looked at Devin, looked at Calvin, looked at me, looked back at Devin, then turned around and called, "Jamie, baby! Come watch the grill. Alex needs to talk to me for a minute," while taking off his apron and trotting toward the Camaro.

"Daddy! I wasn't finished yet."

"I know, baby girl, but Alex and Calvin need me to help them with their ice cream. Start the car, boy!" he mumbled to Calvin as he opened the passenger door.

I hopped in the back seat, Dad breathed a sigh of relief, and Calvin sped off. The only other time I had seen similar relief on a person's face was during a news cast of disaster victims when the rescuers arrived.

"What in the world was Devin talking your ear off about, Dad?" I asked.

"Probably the Mayor Atley. She won't be quiet about him," answered Calvin.

"Lord, yes! She won't stop talking about him. Ever since she led that movement to get Old Man Stuart out of office, she has taken it upon herself to make sure that Mayor Atley makes due on the promises he made to the east side. I guess she heard me complain about Old Man Stuart not keeping promises so much back in the day that now she feels like it's her duty to make sure the new mayor does."

"So, in other words, Unk, this is all Pop's fault," Calvin said with a laugh.

"I'm afraid he's right, Alex. I may have created a monster."

"Well, has he done anything he said he would do, or has he gone straight to ignoring the east side?" I asked.

"Yes and no, son. You probably noticed the new restaurants and stores around here. That's been a good thing. The tourists aren't afraid to come to this side of town like they used to be, so having places to eat and shop over here has brought in a lot of much-needed revenue."

"So what's Devin griping about?"

"Her issue is the crime. This new mayor ran on a platform of bringing resources to the east side, but he promised to put more effort into reducing the crime here as well. You know how your sister is. If you tell her something, you better do it. If you don't, she's going to tell you and anyone who will listen about how you didn't do what you said you were going to do. The east side got really bad when you went off to college, son. She didn't go off to Florida State until after you went off to college, so she saw it start to go down, and it really got to her. A lot of the friends both of you had got caught up in drugs in some way. Some of her friends started taking the drugs that came in, and some of yours started selling them. A few of Devin's friends got cleaned up, but a lot of the ones that got hooked on that stuff are still on it today. Some of the kids I remember you running around with wanted that quick money and ended up dead or in jail. A few kids went missing back then too."

"Really? No one ever told me about that."

"Yeah. A few from your high school if I remember correctly. Don't know if they died or just left, but one minute she was walking the halls with these kids, and the next minute they were gone. I have to admit, even I was kind of spooked by that. Those kids going missing, along with that thing that happened with you and Allen at the beach when you were kids really shook her up. She's turned into this... this...what is that you call her, Calvin?"

"A social justice warrior, Pop"

"Yeah...a social justice warrior, and she's wearing everybody smooth about it."

"Who were these kids that went missing, Dad?"

"You'll have to talk to your sister about that, son. Just do me one favor when you do talk to her about it."

"What's that, Dad?"

"Make sure I'm either out of the house or asleep because I can't go getting dragged into another one of her social justice warrior conversations this week. She's got my nerves all worked up," he said with a laugh.

We crossed the bridge to the west side in search of ice cream. The west side was already nice, but the improvements the new mayor brought in here were much nicer than those on the east side. Many of the beachside shops that I remember as a kid were replaced by corporate stores or franchises. Everything from clothing retailers and restaurants to boat and car dealerships were on the beach now. Even I have to admit that I was very impressed with how it looked in Patrician as a whole but especially on the west side. With all this added grandeur, I could see why Devin was a bit irritated. The types of improvements she wants take time, so do the types of improvements I see on the west side. From the sound of it, though, these improvements took no time at all. I just had to gear up for that conversation with her because I knew once I got her going, I'd be there for a while.

As a kid, I loved this part of the beach. Coronado Street is where most of the seafood restaurants, ice cream, and snow-cone shops used to be. Most of the restaurants are still there, but a lot of those older shops either closed down or were bought out when the business expansion came through. After driving past all the newer developments, it was really good to see Kreemy Kone's ice-cream stand still holding forth. In my eyes, it was the only ice-cream shop that could compete with the Dairy Queen in New Smyrna Beach, and I would literally beg Dad to stop there whenever we came to this side of town. Dad must have heard me getting fidgety in my seat like I used to when I got close to Kreemy Kone's because he told Calvin to pull into their parking lot. I was the first one out of the car. I trotted to the line and ordered the same thing I ordered when I was a kid: a chocolate-covered, double-dipped, soft-serve ice-cream cone. I was eating mine by the time Dad and Calvin got to the line. I gave the girl at the counter a $20 bill and told her to give the change to either Dad or Calvin after they ordered theirs. I sat down and ate my cone on the same metal table and chairs covered by a shade umbrella that I sat on as a kid.

Dad and Calvin walked over with their cones about five minutes later. Calvin loves to hear me tell Air Force stories, so we began to talk about Stratotankers, guns, and Lt. Michelle Paulson (with whom Calvin has been infatuated since he was about six). Telling him that Michelle bought my truck from me reminded me that I had to turn in the Camaro and look for a car to purchase. Dad told me I could use his, but I wanted to get my own car as soon as possible so I didn't impose on Mom and him too much. I was thinking I would want another truck or maybe a Jeep so I could drive on the beach, but I had gotten used to the speed and power of the Camaro. I pulled out my phone and scoured the internet, looking for someone with a sports car to sell.

"Any idea of what you want to buy, son?"

"I really like what this Camaro SS can do, Dad, but not sure if I want to spend that much on a car right now, especially seeing I haven't found a job yet."

"You should get a Camaro just like this one, Unk! How much does one of these costs?"

"Somewhere around $35,000. I need to buy a house too, so I probably won't spend that much on a car."

"Mom says you're cheap, Unk."

"I prefer frugal. At the end of the day, I just need to get from point A to point B."

"I understand that, Unk, but you don't need to drive a bucket. Mom said that you were 'the man' in high school, and all the girls liked you, so you need something fly!"

"First, I'm fly regardless of what I drive. Remember that, nephew! Second, Devin talks too much. Third, if I didn't know any better, your desire for me to have something fly has more to do with you having something nice to borrow from your uncle than with your concern about your uncle having a nice car for himself."

"Nah, Unk, it's not like that," he said while flashing an enormous smile.

Just as he said that, I scrolled to a private seller across town trying to get rid of a car that I wanted to get years ago but always missed out on back in the day: a 2004 Saleen Mustang. It was quite a few years older than I was considering, but with the low miles and price, I had to at least look at this.

"Where is Cloud Street, Dad?"

"That's here on the west side, son. I think it's in one of those new housing developments south of here. Why?"

"Someone out there has a car for sale that I want to look at."

"What are we about to get, Unk?" asked Calvin, rubbing his hands together.

"*I'm* going to look at a Saleen Mustang."

"You ballin' like *that*, Unk? I seriously need to look at going into the Air Force."

"Chill, Calvin," I said with a smile. "It's a Saleen, but it's a little older."

"How much older, son?"

"A 2004."

"That's almost as old as me, Unk! Why are you looking at one so old?"

"I loved that body style for the Mustang, Calvin. Almost bought one back when you were little, but it sold by the time I got to the dealership. I've wanted one ever since. Plus, this one only has ten thousand miles on it, and he's only asking $6,500 for it. Looks like he just listed it an hour ago. It'll be dark in an hour. You guys mind coming to look at it with me now? This one will probably sell fast."

"Hate to spoil the fun, son, but your mother just texted me. Devin is about to drive her crazy, and she's not too happy with me pawning her off on her as I did," Dad said with a laugh.

"Say no more, Dad! We better get you home *fast!*"

As we walked back to the car, I noticed two guys who had been hanging out at the snow-cone shop across from Kreemy Kone's get up from their table and start heading toward us. Dad got into the passenger seat while Calvin walked around to the driver's side. One of the men was a tall Black man with an athletic build. If I were to guess, he played basketball at one time or was a wide receiver in football. The other was a long-haired White man who was nearly the same height as the other man. They jogged across the street with a strange swing to their arms. Their left arms were bent in the normal position you would see when a person jogs, but their right arms were straight which told me they literally had something up their sleeves. I thought to myself, *I know these fools aren't going to try to rob me with my father and nephew in the car.*

"Nice car, man!" said the long-haired man as he positioned himself near the passenger side.

"I wish I had one like it. How 'bout you let me have this one?" said the other man as he allowed a crowbar to slide out of his left sleeve and into his hand while standing at the rear of the car.

"Look, guys, this is a rental, and I'm not about to get into it with you fools over a car that isn't mine. Just let my dad and nephew out of the car, and you can do whatever you want with it."

I moved slowly toward my father's side, taking note of the man turning to face me as he also allowed a crowbar to slide out of his right sleeve into his hand. The man at the back of the car was rather calm as he watched to see what I do. The other man appeared nervous as I slowly walked toward him and Dad, indicating that this was probably his first carjacking. I didn't want any problems, but I quickly prepared myself mentally in the event that something popped off. The dude was jittery with a crowbar in his right hand, which meant that he would likely take a wild side or overhead swing at my head if he got spooked. If that happened, I'd step into the swing, using both hands to secure the wrist of the hand holding the crowbar. A quick elbow to the jaw will hurt but not incapacitate. Follow the elbow with a groin shot with my right hand while continuing to secure the hand holding the crowbar with my left hand. Resecure the wrist of the hand holding the crowbar with both hands and throw him over my hip and shoulder to the ground while still securing the wrist. Place my foot on his right pectoralis muscle while holding the wrist, pull upward sharply and dislocate his shoulder. Quickly take crowbar and throw it at the now-charging second assailant, thereby incapacitating both men. I hoped it didn't come to that.

As I feared, he yelled, "Get back, man!"

"Chill, man. Just going to open the car door to let my dad out. Calvin, go ahead and get out."

"Keep yo ass in that seat, Calvin!" said the man at the back of the car. "I say when you can move."

"I'm just coming over to get my father out of the car."

"I said get the fuck back!" he shouted, and just as I feared, he threw a wild overhead swing at my head.

I stepped into his swing, using both hands to secure the wrist of his hand holding the crowbar. I threw a quick elbow to his jaw, which hurt him but did not incapacitate him. I followed the elbow with a shot to the groin using my right hand while continuing to secure his hand holding the crowbar with my left. I then resecured the wrist of the hand holding the crowbar with both hands and threw him over my hip and shoulder to the ground while still securing his wrist. Placed my foot on his right pectoralis muscle while holding the wrist, pulled sharply upward, and dislocated his shoulder. While he lay there screaming, as I knew he would, the guy from the back of the car ran toward me with his crowbar above his head, ready to swing. I quickly took the crowbar from his friend and threw it, hitting him squarely in the face, immediately knocking him unconscious.

"You okay, Dad?"

"I'm good, son. Thank you."

"Calvin, call the police. Calvin!"

"Yeah, Unk?"

"Call the police, man!"

"Uh-huh. What kind of *Five Deadly Venoms*, Bruce Lee type of shit was that, Unk?"

"Watch your mouth in front of your grandfather, man! What's the matter with you?"

"My bad. Okay, I'll call 'em."

Several police officers arrived and began questioning my account of what happened. Of course, both men said I misunderstood their intentions and that I had attacked them for simply asking questions. The young lady to whom I gave the $20 bill told the officers that what I described was exactly what she witnessed. After speaking with the young lady at Kreemy Kone's, one of the police officers asked me my name.

As I began to say my name, I heard a voice behind me say, "That's Alex Archer. I know that peanut-head anywhere."

There were only two people in the world who would ever say that. One of them was at Fairchild AFB, preparing to move to Florida, and the other was my high school teammate Glen Hixon... Officer Glen Hixon. We ran track together in high school. When we graduated high school, he joined the Marine Corps. He hadn't changed much at all. Same blond hair and tanned skin, like he sits on the beach all day. Still in really good shape too. I always told him that he looked like Captain America without the mask.

"Never met an Air Force guy that could actually throw a punch!"

"I guess you still haven't. I didn't punch him."

We stared at each other dead silent with straight faces for a few moments, which appeared awkward to everyone watching, before we cracked up laughing.

"How ya been, Arch? I ran into Devin a few weeks back, and she told me you were coming back home. Didn't expect to see you like this, but it's good to see you anyway."

"I literally drove in about two hours ago."

"So let me get this straight. You get into town, say hello to a few people, drive to the beach, and start beating the hell outta people in under two hours? If I didn't know any better, I'd swear you were a Marine."

I laughed and caught up with Glen for a few minutes then remembered that I had to get Dad and Calvin home.

"Call me, Glen, so we can finish catching up. I gotta get Dad home and go check on a car before it gets dark."

"Will do, Arch! Here's my card. Sorry for holding him, Mr. Archer!" he said to Dad.

With that, I peeled out of the parking lot, intent on both seeing this Saleen Mustang and keeping Dad out of hot water with Mom. About a mile or so from our house, it dawned on me that I hadn't even called to see if the owner was home. I dialed the number and asked the owner if the car was available. He told me it was and could be viewed. He gave me the address, which I committed to memory: 819 Cloud Street. I pulled up to our house and saw that everyone was still in front, eating and enjoying each other's company. Everyone except Mom. I saw her sitting on the front porch with a look of complete exasperation and Devin sitting next to her with the same look. Dad hopped out and walked toward the front door, trying to avoid the glare that Mom was boring into him. I already knew the answer, but I figured that I would ask anyway to cut the tension.

"What's wrong, Mom?"

"Your sister won't stop running her mouth about this new mayor, and I can't take it anymore! I told her she was going to have to give it a rest, and now she's sitting here with her feelings hurt."

Devin was sitting there, looking like someone whose favorite puppy ran away.

I knew that I might be sorry later, but I blurted out, "Wanna ride with me, Dev? I'm about to look at this car on Cloud Street."

Still pouting, she nodded and started walking to the car.

"It's your turn now, Alex, because we can't take it any-more," she said with a laugh. Dad saw Mom smile, and he kissed her on the cheek. "Don't kiss me, David! You aren't back in my good graces yet! You knew Devin was gonna talk my ear off about this mayor!"

I laughed and headed to the car. Calvin saw his mother coming to the car, so he jumped out and began looking for Mike.

Before he took off, he said to Devin, "Mom! Uncle Alex is a beast! He took on two dudes at the same time at the beach and won! Now he's about to go buy a car! I need to look into joining the Air Force."

"You haven't been here a day yet! Why are you fighting?"

"Not now, Dev! It's not like that. I gotta get to Cloud Street before it gets too dark to see the car!"

"Cloud Street? That new neighborhood by the beach where all the rich people live? What are you buying, a Bugatti?"

"No, I'm not buying a Bugatti, goofy! One of those Saleen Mustangs that I wanted back in '04. It only has ten thousand miles on it, and he's only asking $6,500 for it. He could get at least double for it, so if this is legit, I'm going to buy it."

"Definitely worth a look. That's one of those special types of Mustangs, right?"

"Yep."

"I think one of my classmates bought one of those a few years ago. Had all of those extra decorations and stuff. I don't like sports cars, but this one was really nice!"

"This one is black too."

"Maybe it's the same guy. His name was Jeff Rayless, if I remember."

"I doubt it, Dev. This guy sounded quite a bit older than us."

We turned onto Cloud Street and pulled up to a guard shack as it began to get a little dusky outside. The shack sat in front of two large solid steel doors placed between tall concrete walls. Everything about the design of the walls, doors, and guard shack said the people who lived inside had no desire to be bothered. I can honestly say I have seen military bases that looked more inviting. The guard emerged from the shack with an air about himself that was just as imposing as the gate and wall that he was guarding. It wasn't his size or even the Glock 19 that he made sure was visible as he emerged. It was his eyes. It was his walk. It was the way he asked us what business we had inside. Everything about him was serious business.

"Evening, sir. Who are you here to see?"

"I don't have a name. Just an address. I'm looking at a car that he has for sale."

"What's the address, sir?"

"819 Cloud Street."

Without hesitation the guard said, "Mr. Rayless's residence. Sit here while I call him."

I looked over at Devin, and I could see her gears turning like the inner workings of a grandfather clock. She wasn't spooked, but she did look confused and bothered at the same time. I could see the guard in the shack nod affirmatively before hanging up the phone. He returned to the car window, gave us quick directions to the house, and then returned to the shack to open the gate without saying another word. The gate slowly opened, and we drove in.

To use the word "houses" as a description for where these people lived would be a gross understatement. They were more like mansions or castles. Each one similar to the other but unique as well. As we drove toward Mr. Rayless's house, I asked Devin why she looked so weird when she heard the Rayless name.

She said, "No reason. I just can't really remember the last time I saw or heard anything about Jeff or his girlfriend, Rebecca. I remember them being crazy about each other. I knew his people had money, but not like this! Rebecca was very pretty, but kinda homely. She lived farther east than we did. I don't remember exactly where, but I know it was either in the trailer park or in the projects. I think her last name was Matthews, and she looked mixed: long, brown, spirally hair, tan-skinned, and hazel eyes. Rebecca didn't wear that Ralph Lauren and Hugo Boss that Jeff wore, but you could tell every time he looked at her, it was like he was looking at the most beautiful woman he had ever seen! She did start dressing better when they got together. I'd see him taking her shopping at the mall after school and out to eat on the weekends. They were still together years after we graduated. If you saw one of them, you saw the other. I remember that car so much. No one had one like it. There were Mustangs around, but not ones with all that fancy stuff. Now that I'm thinking about it, he knew Robert really well. This was about ten or so years after I graduated high school, and also when Robert started doing really well at the bank. I think Jeff was in commercial real estate, and Robert would work on his loans or something. Anyway...it was like one minute you'd see them everywhere around the city, and then the next minute, they were gone. There wasn't any noise about it, and it wasn't like I sat around, thinking about them all day. So I guess on that rare occasion when I would be reminded of them for whatever reason, I had it in my mind that they just did like a lot of couples in Patrician who were together that long and got married. People were leaving Patrician left and right back then, so I figured they just got married and moved away. I just wouldn't think that he would leave a car like that behind."

"Maybe Rebecca got pregnant before they moved, and he just left the car with his father when they bought a sedan."

"That still doesn't make sense, Alex. I know he has money, but no one is just going to leave a car with someone when they can sell it or at least trade it in to buy the type of car they need."

"What are you getting at, Dev?"

"Nothing, man! I'm just talking. It's just weird that someone would just walk away from that kind of car. That's all."

I didn't mean to come off snappy to Devin, but I knew she had a point. I just didn't want this conversation to turn into one of her tangents on the way to seeing a car that I was hoping wasn't too good to be true. Being a sports-car lover myself, I couldn't help but think about what Devin said. Why would a person leave a car like this behind?

After a few minutes of meandering through the development, we pulled up to 819 Cloud Street. The estate sat slightly recessed from the others in the development. A cobblestone circle driveway surrounding a fountain allowed you to drive up to the front porch of what had to be one of the largest, most palatial homes I had ever seen. In front of it sat the Saleen Mustang that I had been hoping wasn't too good to be true. The sun was about twenty minutes from setting, so the estate's security lights were beginning to slowly turn on like you see at a stadium.

As we pulled up to the Mustang, Mr. Rayless stepped off the porch and met us as we parked. He was a tall, slender man who appeared to be in great shape in his sixties. A head full of gray hair, none of which was out of place. A very neat and tidy appearance with a confident look about himself, he looked as if he had just stepped out of a country club.

"You must be Mr. Rayless."

"You got it, but call me Edward! And you are..."

"Alex. It's a pleasure to meet you. This is my sister, Devin."

She responded with a smile and a short wave.

"Well...here she is. 2004 Saleen Mustang."

"Sir, I have to ask. Why are the miles so low, and why is it so cheap? Don't get me wrong, I don't want you to hike the price up, but you gotta know you're selling this for a lot less than you can get. Is something wrong with it?"

"Not a thing. I priced it this way because I knew it would move quickly, and I need room in the garage. Here are the keys. Take it around the block. In fact, take it out of the complex and open it up so you can see nothing's wrong with it."

"If you don't mind then, I'd be glad to. I won't be long."

"No worries. I'll be here waiting."

Like a kid on Christmas taking a new toy outside, I cranked it up and took off. The car drove great in the city and even better on the open road. I was sold as soon as I heard that engine growl when I merged onto the freeway. My mind was made up. This Mustang was coming home with me, and what made this even better was the fact that I found it so quickly.

I turned to Devin and said, "This is coming home with me! What do you think?"

"Huh...yeah, bro. It's cool."

Now, anyone who knows Devin knows that a response like that from her meant she had a multiplicity of thoughts bouncing around her head, and something was about to fly out of her mouth whether you liked it or not.

"Look, Devin, I know what you're thinking. Leave this Jeff thing alone. I'm trying to buy this car, and I don't need you messing this up."

"What? I'm not going to mess anything up. All I said is it's just weird that Jeff would leave without this car. We weren't best friends or anything, but I remember how much he loved Rebecca, and I remember how much he loved this car."

"I hear all that, but don't go putting your nose anywhere it doesn't belong."

"Alex...stop! Are you buying the car or not?"

"Whatever, Dev! You and I both know how your mouth can be. Don't start running it when we get back."

She shook her head and let out a big sigh, suggesting I was overreacting. I love my sister, but her mouth has gotten her and me in trouble since we were kids, and I didn't want that mouth ruining this. Part of my issue was that, as much as I don't want admit it, what she was saying sort of made sense. The car hadn't been driven much, and I knew I wouldn't have left a car like this behind.

We pulled back up to the gate, and the guard waved us in. I pulled back up to Mr. Rayless's driveway.

"Edward, I'll take it!"

"I had a feeling you would after I saw how you looked at it when you got out of your car. Speaking of which, you're in a new Camaro. What do you want with this?"

"This is a rental. I just retired from the Air Force and came back to Patrician. Been driving a GMC Sierra for the past couple of years. I don't need four-wheel drive down here, so I figured I'd get a sports car. I wanted a Saleen in 2004 and always missed out on getting one. When I saw this, I had to at least check it out. Why spend thirty-something thousand dollars when I can spend $6,000?"

"It's $6,500," he says.

"I know…but I figured I'd offer you $6,000 and see what you'd say," I said with a grin.

"Tell you what," he said. "You said that you're retired Air Force, right?"

"Yes, sir, I am."

"Meet me in the middle at $6,250, and it's yours."

"Done deal," I said, and we shook hands.

"Did you bring cash?"

"I saw the ad, dropped my father off at home, and drove straight here, so I didn't get the cash. The banks were already closed as well. I have about $300 cash on me. I can give you that to hold it and bring you a cashier's check for $5,950 tomorrow."

"I can do that."

As Edward and I began talking about what I did in the Air Force and his career as a real estate investor, I couldn't help but notice Devin studying the car with a look on her face that I recognized. It was a look she always got before she began putting her nose in places that made people uncomfortable.

I began trying to catch her eye to shut her down without Mr. Rayless noticing, but before I could, she looked in our direction and said, "This must be Jeff Rayless's car. I knew him in high school."

The pit of my stomach dropped to my feet because it was at this point I felt the tone of our interaction change. The smiling face and friendly persona that Edward presented was suddenly replaced with a rather-troubled expression which seemed to mask pain and discomfort.

"I'm so sorry Edward. Did I say something wrong?" Devin asked in an attempt to ease the enormous level of tension now rising.

If looks could kill, my sister wouldn't have dropped dead, but her heart may have skipped a few beats because of how hard I stared at her as I said, "Edward, I hope we didn't cause any trouble."

"No, no…you're fine. Jeff is my son, and I haven't talked to him in quite a long time."

"I am so sorry! I didn't mean to upset you, Mr. Rayless," said Devin.

"It's okay. Really, it is. How could you have known?" He turned to me and asked, "What time should I expect you tomorrow, Alex?"

Still staring at Devin, I replied, "How about 11:00 a.m.? That gives me time to go by the bank. My cousin Robert has been handling my investment and other accounts for years. He'll be in his office tomorrow morning at 10:00 a.m."

"Sounds good. I'll see you tomorrow at 11:00 a.m. I'll put the car back in the garage and take the ad offline. Now if you'll excuse me, I have some packing to do. I'm going out of town for a few days after you and I wrap things up tomorrow."

"No problem, Edward. Have a great night, and thank you."

A little of the graciousness that he had shared began to show through again as he walked us back to the Camaro, but it was clear that Edward was still a bit troubled by whatever emotions and thoughts Devin triggered by doing exactly what I told her not to do.

"Good night, guys," he said as we started the Camaro.

I nodded and waved, still somewhat embarrassed by Devin's question as we began to circle the fountain in the driveway.

"Damn, Devin! You just had to open your mouth, didn't you?"

"Look, don't start, Alex. It just slipped out. My bad. How was I supposed to know?"

We didn't have very far to drive to get back to Mom and Dad's house, but the silence in the car was making the ride back home an awkward one. One thing I've always admired about my little sister is that she is going to be herself, like it or not. This just happens to be one of those "not" times.

"Bro…don't be upset at me. I wasn't trying to bother that man. It's just that going to that house and seeing that car without seeing Jeff or Rebecca was just odd to me."

"I'm not mad, Dev. He said he was fine, so don't worry about it. I'm just buying a car."

"I know you, Alex, and I know your wheels are turning about this, like mine are."

"Maybe so. But I just got home a few hours ago, and whatever is going on between him and his son is their business, not mine, and certainly not yours. I'm going to forget about it and eat some of Dad's barbecue."

CHAPTER 4

The next morning, I called my cousin Robert and told him to cut me a cashier's check from my primary account for the remaining $5,950 that I needed to give Edward. The bank didn't open until 9:00, but as the bank president, Robert was usually there before everyone. He used that time to make sure my check was cut before he got caught up in his daily routine. I was like a kid on Christmas, waking up to open up that big present under the tree that you're 99 percent sure is the present you had been asking for. You know what it is, but you just can't wait to get your hands on it. Devin had apologized again when we got back to Dad and Mom's last night, but to avoid her putting her foot in her mouth again, I asked Mom and Dad to take me to get the check and pick up the car. They were more than happy to help after hearing how uncomfortable Devin's prying made Edward feel. For helping me pick up my car and making sure I had a great "welcome home" get-together last night, I promised to treat them to breakfast.

Mom couldn't help but laugh as I explained how annoyed I was with Devin asking Edward if her old classmate owned that car.

"You knew what you were getting into when you invited her to go with you," said Mom. "Don't expect me to feel bad for you. That's what you get for letting your father pawn her off on me when she was in the middle of one of her rants."

"My bad, Mom. Dad told me she has become quite the social justice warrior recently because of the crime on the east side. Doesn't look like it's just the east side anymore either."

"What do you mean?"

"A couple of guys tried to steal the Camaro last night when Dad, Calvin, and I were at Kreemy Kone's yesterday."

"Really? That must be what Calvin was running around talking about at the house last night. Talking about his Uncle Alex being a bad ass. I take it all that military training came in handy."

"You could say that," I said while looking at Dad with a wink.

(A little secret that Dad and I have is that he used to sneak and teach me to box and wrestle when I was a kid. Mom hated the idea of me resorting to violence, so she would have had a fit had she had known he had been teaching me to fight since kindergarten. The military combat training came very easily to me because of it.)

Mom and I continued to talk about the incident at Kreemy Kone's last night.

"I hate to say it, son, but I can't say I'm surprised about what happened last night at Kreemy Kone's."

"Why do you say that, Mom?"

"That beachfront area has become kinda bad, son. It's not the fun little place you used to go to get ice cream anymore. A lot of bad stuff goes on out there. It used to be a place to go with your family and have a good time. Now there's no telling what you'll see if you go down there. You saw the car thieves, of course, but you must have been too caught up in your ice cream to notice the hookers and addicts down there."

"I guess so. Kreemy Kone's still has its hold on me, I suppose."

"I know you can handle yourself, son, but just be careful when you go down there."

"Yes, ma'am."

"It's about time to go pick up your car, son," Dad said.

"Oh yeah! Let me get the check."

After paying the check, I called Edward to let him know we were on our way, and we headed toward Cloud Street after we dropped off the rental car. As we headed toward Edward's house, Mom began doing what mothers do; she began asking me every question under the sun. Most of the questions about things like marriage or girlfriends, I could either dodge or dance around, but Mom had a way of asking questions that provoked a lot of thought.

"Baby, you found this car really fast. What are you going to do now that you're home? I'm very glad to have you back home, but I was surprised to hear you were coming back. All you talked about before you went off to school was leaving Patrician. Are you going to be okay being back home, son?"

"I thought long and hard before I decided to come back, Mom. Believe it or not, I actually began to miss Patrician. Fairchild was great, but being away from family was kind of tough sometimes. I just know that I need to be here right now."

"Okay, son. It's just good to have you home, and I want you to be fine here. Patrician is metropolitan and has even more to offer now than it did when you were in high school. Just wanting to be sure that it has what you need."

"What do you mean, Mom?"

"Baby, you've been all over the world. You've done and seen so much. I would just hate for you to have to leave again to find something fulfilling."

"I'm good, Mom, and being home is good too."

What I don't think Mom understands is that being home with no major responsibilities is something I have been looking forward to. I've saved and invested well, so I don't have to go rush and find something to do right away. I talked to a few airlines about flying for them, but I'm in no hurry. In my mind, I have two responsibilities, one of which I just added to my plate: enjoying the present and making sure that Mom knows I'm not looking to leave Patrician. I owe her that.

We approached the gate and were met at the guard shack by the same stoic security guard from last night. Edward must have told him we were on our way because he waved us in as soon as he saw my face in the back seat.

"This is a high-dollar area back here, son. What are you buying, a Rolls Royce?" asked Dad.

"Dad, you sound as bad as Devin. No, I'm not buying a Rolls. Just buying a Mustang that I wanted back in the day. His house is the one past the ninth hole with the fountain in the circle driveway."

We pulled up next to the fountain and saw Edward out front, wiping down the Mustang.

"Morning, Alex! These your folks?"

"Yes, sir!" I said proudly. Mom, Dad, and I exited the car as Edward walked toward us. "These are my parents, David and Jamie Archer. You didn't have to wax the car, Edward."

"It's no trouble," he said as he greeted my parents. "You've raised a fine young man. I really have enjoyed getting to know him."

"Thank you so much! So glad that he decided to come home," Mom said.

"Well, here she is. Shined up and ready to go."

I handed him the cashier's check, and Edward handed me the keys.

"We're not going to hold you up, Edward. I know you're going out of town today, so we'll get out of your hair."

"My trip actually got delayed a few hours, Alex, so I'm not in too big of a rush right now. I didn't get fully packed anyway, so it worked out well. If you and your folks have a little time, I'd love to show you around."

"That'd be great! Mom, Dad…you guys okay with that?"

"Sure. This is a beautiful place. We'd love to see it."

I've traveled the world and seen some of the most beautiful homes imaginable, but I would have to say that Edward's estate was among the nicest and most extravagant I had ever seen. For one thing, no Florida estate would be complete without palm trees; several tall ones stood next to his mansion. To the left of the house were several beautifully manicured acres of land with mossy southern live oaks and magnolia trees scattered throughout. You could see that toward the back of the acreage was a nice-sized gazebo. Edward talked about how he originally wanted to have a pond there but didn't want to run the risk of giving alligators a place to hide out on his land. He walked us back to the front of the house and walked us in through the front door of his Mediterranean-style home. A huge staircase met us at the foyer when we walked in. The huge stone fireplace with high ceilings in the main room, gourmet kitchen, media room, library, wine cellar, and dens, exuded opulence. The rear of the house was amazing. It was set up resort-style. There was a massive pool and waterfall, with Mediterranean-style verandas. His property sat at the rear of the community near the back wall. He had a special entrance built into the wall which allowed him to connect a dock to his property. Because of the security risk, he told us that he'd had to agree to pay for someone to secure that part of the wall.

"What do you do for a living, Edward?" Dad asked.

"I do a little real estate."

"Looks to me like you do more than just a little." Dad chuckled. "This is beautiful, Edward."

"Thank you, sir." Edward turned to me and asked, "You still enjoying being home, I take it?"

"Absolutely. Patrician has a lot more going on now than it did when I was younger, so I am really enjoying it," I said as I looked reassuringly at Mom. "I'm in no major hurry, but I do want to find something to do so I don't get on my parents' nerves too much during the day."

"I'm sure they won't mind having you around after you being gone so long. Which reminds me, you're a pilot, right?"

"Yes, I am."

"You might want to check into this private charter company near the beach."

"Really? Where do they fly, and what kind of planes do they use?"

"Can't tell you much about the kinds of planes they fly. I'm not a flyboy like you, so all I know is that they fly. What I can tell you is they fly mainly to the Bahamas and the Tranquil Islands in the gulf. They're only about an hour or so by plane off the gulf coast, so it's a quick flight."

"Wasn't there a cruise ship or ferry that took people out there?"

"There was up until about ten years ago. The man who owned it retired and turned it over to his son who really didn't know how to run a company. Last I heard, the son sold the boats and started renting jet skis out to people. People still wanted to go to the Tranquil Islands, so a couple of guys around here who had planes started flying people out to the islands for money. Those guys joined up and started a company that has really boomed. I'm going to the Tranquil Islands this weekend, and I fly with them a lot. Two of their pilots just moved on, and they're looking for someone to take over for them. I can put a word in for you if you'd like. Two of the owners have had to take over those flights, and they're looking to get out of that as soon as they can."

"Yeah, if you don't mind. That'd be great, Edward."

"Done. I'll let them know that you're interested tonight. In fact, I have your number in my caller ID. I can call you when I get to the airstrip and let you all set something up."

"Even better. I'll be looking for your call. Thank you."

"Glad to help. Well, I'm going to get a few things done around here before I get to the airstrip. Thanks for letting me show you around, and thanks for sharing your folks with me."

Edward escorted us to the driveway and waved as he walked back to his porch. Mom and Dad jumped in their car, and I jumped in my Saleen. I told my parents I was going for a drive and that I'd see them back at the house. You would think that a guy who's been driving the country for the past three weeks would be tired of driving, but that wasn't the case. I dropped the top, hit the highway, and opened it up for a little bit. I was going to go up to Tampa until I got a call from Robert.

"What's going on, cuz? Did everything work out with the car?"

"Yeah, man. Worked out perfectly! Thanks for having that check ready for me."

"Aw, man, that's what I do. Where you at right now? Wanna grab some lunch? It's on me. I just want to hang out with your big head for a little while."

"That's a plan. Let me turn around, and I'll be there in about fifteen minutes."

I hit the next exit and headed to the bank. I couldn't help but think about how good it was to see Robert doing so well at the bank. It's not surprising—just good to see. So many people we grew up with who stayed in Patrician aren't doing so well. I was glad to see a success story from our side of the tracks, and especially good seeing it from my family.

First Patrician Bank sits on the corner of Gulf Intercoastal Way and Canal Street. As I pulled up to the red light at the intersection, I saw Robert standing outside, smiling and talking to people as they came into the bank. I revved the engine to get his attention and got him to turn to see the car at the light. He looked as the light turned green. His smile turned to a look of confusion mixed with curiosity as I drove up.

"So you made all this fuss and had me running around this morning for this giant Hot Wheels car," he said with a laugh.

"Don't start, Rob! You know I like fast cars."

"Fast and old. Hey…it's your money, so I guess you can buy what you want when you don't have a wife and kids. I thought that check today was for a down payment on something new."

"That was the original plan, but I always liked these, and when I saw one with only ten thousand miles for this cheap, I had to look."

"A bit old for me, but I can see why you got it," he said as he walked around the Mustang.

As he continued to look at my car, I couldn't help but notice that Robert's look of confusion and curiosity began to change. It was almost as if the car had begun to trouble him. To stop the moment from becoming any more awkward, I told him to hop his butt in the car so we could go eat. After Devin asking questions that I told her not to last night and Robert walking around looking like some nutcase, my excitement about buying this car was slowly going down the drain.

It was about 2:30 when we pulled up to The Dunes Bar and Grill on Gulf Intercoastal Way. It's one of those newer restaurants that Mayor Atley helped to bring in. Great atmosphere inside. Friendly staff, and judging from the aromas coming from the kitchen, I knew the food would be good. Robert visited there a lot, so he knew just about everyone in the restaurant. I spent the first fifteen minutes or so watching Robert talk to various people who came up to the table.

When things finally settled down, I asked, "So let's have it. What's your real issue with my car? You spooked by it too?"

"What do you mean?"

"You looked like you had seen a ghost when you saw me sitting in it. Between you and Devin acting like a couple of clowns about my car, I'm starting to not even want the thing anymore."

Now, of course, I didn't mean that. Truth be told, I love my family, but I couldn't care less if those two knuckleheads liked my car of not. Both of them being so spooked about this car did sort of pique my curiosity. So knowing how Robert likes to talk, I just figured I would throw the bone out there and see how much he would gnaw on it.

"Well, cuz, to be honest with you, seeing that car again was kind of like seeing a ghost."

"What do you mean by that?"

"Anyone around our ages that cares to remember knows that car belonged to Jeff Rayless."

"Yeah…and?"

"Well, the guy just up and disappeared one day. He and his fiancée. Rebecca or something like that. Really pretty girl with hazel eyes. It was like one day they were here, and the next day *poof*…gone. Now, your big head shows up driving his old car that doesn't look a day older than the last time it was seen on the road. Just makes you think. What the hell happened to them?"

"So he was engaged? Devin just said that Rebecca was his girlfriend."

"No, they were engaged. I got to know him pretty well when I started approving his loan applications. His father, Edward, helped him get into commercial real estate, and he started to do really well for himself. He was crazy about that girl, and he was crazy about that car. I remember him asking me what I thought about the ring he bought her for their engagement. He spent some serious bread on it too. I think it was something like a three-carat diamond. He told me that he had the stone imported from overseas somewhere, and the setting was custom-made for her."

"Okay, so no big deal. They probably got married and moved without making a big deal about it and announcing it to the world. She was probably pregnant, and they needed a new car."

"I doubt it."

"Why?"

"Because he had just been approved for a business loan to develop two new shopping centers on the beach. He had every single space in both shopping centers preleased and was going to make a killing on that project! Who do you know would walk away from something like that? Would you, Alex?"

"Hell no!"

"Okay, so now do you see why it's weird to see this car just pop up after around fifteen years of being nowhere in sight? Where the hell did you find it anyway?"

"His father, Edward, put it up for sale online."

"So nobody's seen Jeff or Rebecca for all this time, and his dad has just had the car sitting in garage for fifteen years? Does that not sound just a tad bit strange to you, Alex?"

"Maybe…but that's not my business. All I know is a man had a car for sale that I wanted. I had the money to buy it, and I bought it."

"I guess. It's just one of those things that people around here look at as a question that needs to be answered but that people are too scared to ask. There hasn't been a peep from him or Rebecca in over a decade. No ten-year high school reunion, social media accounts…nothing. By now, you would usually hear about someone seeing them somewhere. There's none of that."

"I'm telling you, man, he probably just eloped with ol' girl and moved to Jacksonville or something. Anything more than that, I'm not concerning myself with. I just got here, and I don't know these people from a can of paint. Now, can we order? Or are you gonna sit here and keep trying to be a Black Sherlock Holmes?"

"Shut up, man!" he said with his booming laugh.

Our waitress came over to take our order. Robert ordered crab legs, and I ordered my usual fish and chips, my typical choice whenever I eat seafood. I'm a creature of habit when it comes to food, so it never takes me long to order. We continued catching up and reminiscing about childhood good times we had growing up in Patrician. Despite the great food and conversation, I couldn't help but think about what Robert had told me about these two people that I had never laid eyes on. As much as I tried to forget it or not admit it, a man and his fiancée disappearing a day or so after signing papers for a project that would have netted him millions and millions of dollars was a bit odd. The harder I tried to forget it, the more the story Robert told me about Jeff and his fiancée etched itself in my mind.

"You thought about what you want to do now that you're back in good ol' Patrician?" Robert asked. "You know you can always work with me at the bank, right?"

"Thanks, cuz, but I can't do a bank. I need to move around. Being locked up in a building all day would drive me batty."

"So what are you gonna do?"

"I'm not a hundred percent sure. I have a few airlines that have talked to me about flying for them, but I got a lead today about a charter airline service that travels to the Bahamas and Tranquil Islands. Two pilots just moved on, and they need to replace them fast. I'm supposed to get a call from one of the owners this afternoon sometime. That sounds more like the pace I want to go. Fly when needed versus flying under orders. It's retirement time for me, and I'm not trying do some regimented schedule."

"I can definitely understand that. How'd you hear about it?"

"The man who sold me the car told me about it."

"Damn, Alex, you just can't get enough of those people, can you?"

"So what? Am I supposed to not look into it?"

"No, I'm not saying that. I'm just saying, be careful."

"Be careful of what?"

"Nothing in particular. I'm just saying be careful, that's all."

I couldn't help but feel that Robert was telling me something without directly telling me something. That's unlike him though. He may be this smiling, jovial kind of guy, but he's very direct and just says what needs to be said. Maybe I was overthinking, but it sure seemed like there was something else he really wanted to say. For now, though, I decided I'm going to hear this charter service out and make a decision from there.

After Robert finished his second serving of crab legs, he asked the waitress to bring the check. The same multitude of people Robert spoke to on the way to our table spoke to him as we were leaving. We finally got outside and into the car.

"Come on, Al! Not all of us are retired and living the good life. Some of us still have to work," he said with a laugh. "What are you about to get into now, Alex?"

"Nothing much. Going to head over to Kreemy Kone's and then back to Mom and Dad's. They're enjoying me being home, but I have to find me a place soon. I'm too old to do the move-back-home thing, so I'll probably do some house-hunting too."

"I don't blame you. Can't bring a lady to your parents' house, can you? Speaking of which, I just found out that Rayna moved back into town last week. Jessica has been helping her get settled in every day since she got back. She's been in banking for the past ten years, so I got her a job in the lending department at the bank when she told Jessica she wanted to move back home. The first person she asked about was ol' big head Alex Archer," he said with a laugh. "I thought for sure you two would have gotten back together by now."

"Mind your business," I said as we pulled up to the bank. "Thanks for lunch, Rob. I'll let you know what happens with the charter company. Tell Rayna I said hello."

"Oh, you know I will," he said while smiling as though he was expecting me to say that.

I turned left onto Canal Street and made a beeline to Kreemy Kone's. On the way there, I couldn't help but continue to think about why Robert told me to be careful when I talked to the charter company. It was going to take a little more prying, but I was bound to get Robert to talk about why he looked and sounded so weird when I talked about Edward, my car, and flying with this charter company. I've known him all my life, and I know when he's not being straight up about something. This was one of those times.

I ordered a large vanilla-twist soft-serve cone double-dipped in chocolate. After paying for it, I went to sit at the same spot that Dad, Calvin, and I had sat last night. Like last night, I was eating my ice cream when I began to feel like someone was watching me. The uneasiness caused me to look around in an attempt to find its source.

A few moments passed when I noticed a woman staring at me as she walked up from the motel next to Kreemy Kone's.

"What's good here?" she asked with a smile.

Only a blind man wouldn't be able to see how absolutely gorgeous this woman was. So gorgeous, for a split second, I almost didn't notice that my ice cream was starting to drip on my fingers.

I held up my cone and said, "You can't go wrong with a large vanilla-twist soft serve double-dipped in chocolate."

"Looks good. Care if I join you after I order mine?"

"Sure."

"Thanks," she said as she stepped in line to order.

The combination of my personality and training as an Air Force pilot has turned me into a person who pays attention to detail. This woman was tall with shoulder-length black hair. The fact that she was in Florida during the summer dressed in sleeves and leggings suggested she had recently relocated from someplace cold. Despite all her beauty, she didn't appear very confident in herself. I could hear her voice trembling slightly through her thick northeastern accent. I would like to think that her nervousness was due to my devastatingly handsome looks, but I knew better than that.

Desperation has a certain look and sound—and both were emanating from her like heat coming from an oven during a long day of cooking in a small kitchen. As she stood there ordering, I thought of how out of place she looked. She was tall, with smooth mahogany skin, light-brown eyes, and wore a very sweet-smelling perfume. On her face was a superficial smile likely put on to hide fear, pain, or a little of both. Judging from her height, walk, and build, she was an athlete, either now or at some point in her life. She got her cone and returned to my table, smiling the best she could.

Before she could start laying it on me, I asked her, "Why do you look so bothered every time the guy at the other end of the seating area looks at you?"

"What guy?"

"Don't play dumb. The guy at the end of the seating area trying to pretend he's not watching your every move? I like to think that I am a pretty handsome guy, but why's a pretty young lady like you trying to talk to a forty-year-old guy? What are you…about twenty-five? However old you are, you're nervous as hell right now, and you got even more nervous when I mentioned that bum at the end of the seating area. You in some kind of trouble?"

I don't know what possessed me to ask that question. I usually do my best to avoid trouble when it comes my way, but something about the fear in this girl's eyes made me ask. I get on Devin's case all the time about sticking her nose where it doesn't belong. Still, as much as I hate to admit it, whatever is in her DNA that causes her to try to right wrongs that she sees is in mine as well and causes me to try to help people when I see them in trouble. I've never liked to see a person in need, and that has sometimes gotten me in situations I didn't want to be in. Something told me I just did it again.

Against my better judgment, I took a deep breath and said in a low tone, "Look normal and smile, but answer my question: are you in trouble with this guy? Take my hand if you are." With tears beginning to well up in her eyes, she reached across the little table and rubbed my hand as she grabbed it and held it tightly. Her hands began to tremble and sweat. With another deep breath, I said, "Okay, follow my lead. I assume that you work out of the motel you just walked out of." She nodded. "That's a nasty-ass hotel," I said as we walked past the guy at the end of the seating area. "I don't get down like that. It's five-star for me or no star at all, baby."

"What are you doing? They're gonna follow us," she whispered nervously.

"They? How many does 'they' mean?"

"There are three I've seen. They told me they have eyes watching me on the street and in the motel."

"That's what I figured."

"So what are we gonna do?"

"I'll let you know when I know."

"Oh my god! Are you serious?" she whispered.

"Hey… I was just eating an ice-cream cone. You came to my table, remember?"

We continued walking toward the nicer hotels away from where I would think the people handling her would be posted up to watch her. I put my arm around her and pretended to whisper in her ear so I could get a quick glimpse behind me to see if we were being followed. In the distance, I could see the guy who was at the end of the seating area at Kreemy Kone's begin to follow us. He wasn't walking anxiously but was trying to keep pace enough for us to not get out of his line of sight. To our right, I could see a blue sedan begin to keep pace with us as well. The nicest hotel nearest us was the Ocean Harbor Hotel on Coronado Street. We walked to the intersection that was perpendicular with the direction the blue sedan was traveling. As the sedan approached the intersection, I got a quick glimpse inside the car and saw two people. The driver was Latino, and the guy in the passenger seat was Black. We continued down the sidewalk on Coronado Street and entered the Ocean Harbor Hotel lobby. We noticed a restaurant inside to the right, so we went in and sat at the bar. I sat facing the door so I could see if the guys in the blue sedan would follow us in.

To ease the ever-rising tension that was escalating by the second, and to keep my mind working on figuring out the next step, I said, "With all of this going on, I don't even know your name."

"It's Marissa. Marissa Johnson."

"Where are you from, Marissa?"

"Bridgeport, Connecticut."

"Was I right about your age? About twenty-five?"

"Twenty-four, actually."

We were seated at the far side of the bar, facing the entrance. The lobby was probably around fifty feet away from our side of the bar. Just as I began asking Marissa about how she ended up in Patrician, I could hear the sliding glass doors open at the front entrance. I quietly instructed Marissa to keep looking at me and to relax as she talked. No sooner than I said that, the two men from the sedan appeared in the lobby of the bar. They frantically walked in but seemed to relax once they noticed Marissa sitting with me at the bar. To not look too obvious, the two men sat at the bar on the opposite end from us and ordered a couple of beers. Despite them sitting there and glancing over at us periodically, Marissa did a good job pretending to be relaxed and not making it obvious she was trying to get away from them. A few minutes later, the guy from the seating area at Kreemy Kone's joined them and ordered a beer as well. So here I sat now, stuck between the proverbial rock and a hard place. Between me and the lobby door sat three guys who were forcing this girl to do things that she didn't want to do. A girl who, out of all the people at Kreemy Kone's, came up to me and somehow got me to help her get away from these bums. I had two choices: calmly walk out and get a room to take Marissa while we figured something out or walk up to the biggest one of the three and beat his ass. The more I thought about it, the more upset I became. How dare these bastards force someone into a lifestyle like this? Just as I was about to pick choice number two, my phone rang.

"Hello, Alex… Edward Rayless. I've got Jack Parker, owner of Patrician Gulf Charters on the line. You got a minute?"

"Absolutely! Let me step out into the lobby. I'm checking into a hotel for the night."

While on the phone, I took Marissa by the hand and stepped out into the lobby past the three guys at the bar who were watching and listening to my conversation.

"Mr. Archer. This is Jack Parker. I understand you are a pilot."

"Yes, sir, I am."

"Edward says you flew something big in the Air Force, so I'm sure you can handle anything in our fleet. What'd you fly?" he asked while I walked toward the hotel's check-in desk.

"I flew KC-135 Stratotankers, sir. What kind of equipment does your company operate with?"

"Nothing that damned big, that's for sure."

While he began to describe the planes in their fleet, I mouth to the front-desk attendant that we needed a room for two, and I handed her my bank card. I gave a quick glance at the bar to see what the three goons were doing. Our act appeared to be working as I observed the guys at the bar watching the bar television and waiting for us to go upstairs.

"We need someone to take over a run to the Tranquil Islands. Not too sure how familiar you are with the Tranquils, but it's a short flight, about an hour long. You'll have anywhere from two to six people onboard during the flight. At most, two runs a day, and that's rare. On days when things run late, you can stay overnight on the island. Food and lodging are covered when you do. If you come by and like what you see, we can talk money. Sound like anything you'd be interested in?"

"Definitely!"

"Great! We're heading out to the Tranquils tonight. I'll be back at the airstrip near Edward's housing development late morning. I'll call you when I land so we can meet up and I can show you around. Sound good?"

"Sounds great! I look forward to your call tomorrow."

The front-desk attendant handed me the key cards to the room, and we headed toward the elevator.

As we rode up to the fifteenth floor, Marissa asked, "What do we do now?"

"Look, I've never done anything like this before. How does this work?"

"You were supposed to be my first customer. I've never done this either. Being here probably throws things off a little bit.

"How so?"

"They told me they would come by the room to collect the money after they saw the person I brought leaving the room. I watched them as we were getting on the elevator, and they didn't see us get on."

"Okay. I have a cop friend that I can call. Go in the room and lock the door. Open it for no one. I have a key so there's no reason for me to knock. Sit here quietly and stay away from the door."

I grabbed the ice bucket from the hotel room and called my high school teammate, Glen Hixon, as I went back down the elevator.

"Glen! I'm in a situation, man."

"You okay? Where are you?"

"I'm okay for now. I'm at the Ocean Harbor Hotel. There are three guys sitting at a bar. I think they're human traffickers."

"How do you know?"

"It's a long story, but trust me, they are."

"I'm around the corner. I'll be there in two minutes. Stay on the phone with me, Arch. Describe them to me."

"One Black male, one Latino male, one White male. Mid-thirties, T-shirts and jeans on all three. They should be sitting at the bar when you arrive."

"Okay. I'm pulling up and calling a couple of plain-clothes officers to come and assist. I'm trusting you, Arch. You sure about what you're telling me?"

"I wouldn't call you if I weren't, man."

I got back to the ground floor and noticed that two of the guys were still at the bar, but one was not. I did see that the two remaining guys at the bar were watching me. To keep up the appearance of a guy and a girl going to a hotel room for a good time, I headed toward the ice machine next to the bathroom. As I got close to the machine, the third guy exited the bathroom and ran right into me.

"Excuse me."

"No, excuse me," I responded as I proceeded to the ice machine.

He quickly walked back to the bar, glancing back at me once he got back to his two friends. The Latino approached me.

"How long you gonna be with her, man?" he asked. "You one of those guys that's gonna need us to come back in the morning, or can we just wait in the lobby?"

"With who?"

"Don't play dumb, fool! You know."

"I don't think that's any of your damned business, man."

"Best believe everything she does is my business. Just make sure she has my money when you're done."

The words hadn't completely left his lips before I heard, "Patrician Police! You're under arrest for pimping and pandering." With guns drawn, two plainclothes officers moved in on the men at the bar with a third officer coming up next to them from the opposite end of the bar.

As I began to back away, Glen walked in and asked, "You okay, Arch?"

"Yeah, man, I'm good. Glad to see you though."

The officers arrested the men and took them out of the hotel.

"Damn, Arch! You're two for two!"

"Don't start with me, Glen," I said with a laugh.

"No, I'm serious. Come to find out that the two guys you beat down last night had prints that matched a string of car thefts and other crimes stretching all the way to

South Carolina. I'm sure when we look into these three, we'll find they're linked to quite a bit more than just the prostitution."

"This is crazy! Patrician has gotten kinda grimy, hasn't it?"

"You have no idea, Arch! Since you left, a lot of crime has crept in slowly but steadily. I'm not just talking your auto theft and break-ins. I'm talking about that lowlife, sleazy stuff that you see here. Old Man Stuart used to talk tough about crime, but when the rubber met the road, he just turned his head to it. I did a lot of complaining about it when I came back from serving in the Corps. One day I told myself to stop complaining about it and do something, so I joined the police force. I'm glad when we make busts like this one, but the truth is, I honestly am beginning to feel like I'm wasting my damned time. You bust one, and he either gets bonded out or two more take his place. And I'm starting to believe that this new mayor is Old Man Stuart in a younger package."

"Yeah. My sister, Devin, has been giving my family and me an earful about all of this on the political end. Hearing this coming from you on the front line drives her point home even more."

"My plainclothes officer who slid in close to those guys at the bar heard everything they said to you about the woman. Where is she?"

"I got a room upstairs. She's up there." The head tilt and frowned eyebrows (similar to a puppy trying to better hear its master) that Glen gave me let me know what I said came out very wrong. "Glen...come on, man. Not like that. These guys were on our asses like stink on shit, and I had to think fast. I rented a room and left her there to get her away from them."

"Oh…okay," he said with a sigh of relief. "How did you end up in this trick bag in the first place, Arch?"

"I was at Kreemy Kone's, eating an ice-cream cone, and she came up to me nervous as hell while trying to pick me up. When I saw one of those goons watching her every move, I figured something was up. I asked her if she was in trouble, and she said yes."

"I get your instinct kicked in and you took action, Arch, but next time, call me before anything gets started."

"Hopefully, there won't be a next time."

"Yeah, right! This is just day two of you being home. I can only imagine what happens tomorrow." He chuckled. "Let's go talk to her and get some more information."

Glen and I headed to the elevator and up to the fifteenth floor. When we arrived at the room, I keyed the door and announced myself. Marissa sat, cowering in the corner on the floor. Tears of joy and relief streamed down her face when she saw Glen come around the corner behind me. The only words she could get out were, "Thank you. Thank you," and she said it over and over again in trembling whisper.

"Ma'am," Glen said, "I know you've been through a lot, and it may take you a minute, but I need some information about what happened. Do you need a little more time?"

She looked up with a sad and weary but willing look and said, "No, sir. I'm fine. What information do you need?"

"Let's start with your name and where you're from?"

After giving Glen her name and origins, Marissa began to tell us the story of how a young woman who had never left Connecticut somehow ended up in Patrician, Florida. She said it all began when she left Connecticut and met a man who showed her a lot of interest and attention at a really dark time in her life. Her father, who she described as her rock, was killed in a drug deal gone bad. She said he had been taking care of her on his own since she was six years old. Her mother left them when her father lost his job in steel distribution. To make ends meet, she said, he started selling marijuana on the side. It wasn't long before the money that he was making selling weed became too good to stop selling it. Things had returned to normal and even improved to better than normal she said, so she and her father had resigned to the fact that selling weed and making money was their new normal.

Everything was good until his partner told him that he wanted to expand into selling cocaine. She said her father was uneasy about it because he was making good money with weed and didn't really see a need to do anything else. He ignored his gut feeling about it and went along with it to keep his relationship with his partner strong. Her last memory of her father was him walking out of the front door, saying, "See you in a second, baby girl. Daddy's gotta go get this money." He normally would call her after he handled his business. She knew something was wrong when two hours went by, and she heard no word from him. She called and texted him repeatedly and got no answer from either. Another hour passed, and she got a phone call from her father's partner, telling her to leave the house because her dad had been shot, and some guys were coming to the house to get the money that he had stashed away in the basement. He told her to meet him at the park two blocks away so he could make sure she was safe. She said she took off out of the house like a bat out of hell. When she got about a block away from the park, she said she got a really bad feeling in her gut, like something horrible was about to happen. She doubled back but took a different route back home. She hid in the shadow of the alley across the street from her house. A few moments later, she saw a car pull up in front of her house—a car she knew very well. Her father's partner pulled up in front of the house and let two men out. Everything came together when she saw the men enter the house with a key instead of with force. She knew that her father had been set up; even worse, she knew he was dead. Her father would never have given his keys to anyone for any reason, especially with his only daughter in the home alone.

After her father's partner watched the men enter the house, he drove off and called Marissa to make sure that she was at the park. Instead of answering the call, she crushed her phone, threw it in a storm drain, and waited for the men to leave. Her father told her to always keep cash hidden in a spot where she could just grab it and run in the event that something ever happened to him. When the men left with two full duffle bags, she quickly entered the house, pulled up the loose floorboard under her bed, grabbed the cash, and quickly left the house. He always put some money in her stash spot after he made a run; by the time she grabbed it, there was $12,500 under her floor. She made her way to the bus station and bought a ticket to Washington, D.C.

$12,500 is a decent amount of money, but after renting an apartment, buying a cheap car, and paying bills for a few months, that money began to run out pretty fast. Her father's friends, who promised to look out for her in the event that something happened to him, did not follow through even when she called for help. She knew she needed to start working before her money ran completely out, so she took a job as a makeup artist in Crystal City, just outside of D.C. in Virginia. A few weeks went by, and things began to look up a little, but the pain of not having her father around anymore continued to grow. The man who had anchored her was now gone, and she had no one to turn to. She had left Bridgeport without telling anyone, and trusted no one there to keep her location quiet, so with no one other than coworkers to connect with, she grew very lonely in D.C.

That all changed one day when she was at work in Crystal City. She said that while finishing up a woman's face, she was asked to fill in at the perfume counter in the store. She loved perfume and was very knowledgeable about the products, so it wasn't uncommon for the supervisor in that area to ask her to fill in when one of the normal girls was in the bathroom or at lunch. A few minutes after she arrived at the counter, a man she described as the most handsome man she had ever laid eyes on walked up to perfume counter: six feet three inches, athletically built, caramel-complexioned skin, with hazel eyes, a nicely groomed beard, and short wavy hair. The weather was still chilly, so he was wearing a brown leather jacket, cream-colored ribbed turtleneck sweater, dark rinsed jeans, and camel-colored boots. His diamond-studded gold watch caught her eye as much as his looks and clothes. She said she was mesmerized when he started talking to her about wanting to pick up a fragrance for his mother's birthday. After showing him several fragrances, he asked her what her favorite fragrance was. When she told him, he purchased two and told her that she could have one if she went to dinner with him tomorrow. He went on to explain that he had no other expectations than dinner and that she could just meet him at the restaurant of her choice, regardless of the price. She said no, but he persisted and told her that he would hold on to the bottle of perfume in hopes that she would change her mind. If she didn't, the man said he would give it to his sister. With a wink, he walked away and waved goodbye.

The next day he showed up at the same time he showed up the day before, only now he was in a business suit and overcoat. The perfume was gift-wrapped with a bow.

He walked up to the perfume counter and asked, "Is Marissa here today?" to which the perfume counter clerk replied, "Yes, she is. She's over at the makeup counter."

After hearing her name, she said she looked up and saw him walking over with a gift-wrapped box. As he approached, she could see the perfume counter supervisor behind him, gawking and giving her the thumbs-up signal.

Hiding her smile as best she could, she asked, "You actually showed up?"

"Of course," he responded, "I'm a man of my word. Now, are you going to join me for dinner, or do I have to make up a reason for why I bought my sister the same perfume that I bought our mother?"

She said her gut told her to stick to her laurels and trust no one she didn't know, but the months of loneliness combined with the flattery of such a handsome man respectfully asking her on a date made his proposition a difficult one to resist.

After a few moments of him standing with a patient, closed-mouth smile, and the other counter girls nosily and obviously waiting for her response, she said, "I don't go on dates with men who don't tell me their names."

"Wow… I didn't tell you my name, did I? I guess I was distracted by your smile. My name's Tyson. Tyson Lawrence. Do I qualify now, Marissa?"

"I guess so. So where do you plan to take me?"

"The choice is yours, Marissa."

"I'll leave that up to you, Tyson. You can tell a lot about a man based on where he takes a woman on a first date," she said.

"Meet me at Fiona Rose by the river. Is 7:00 okay? I will be finished with my meetings for the day."

"I'll see you then."

"I look forward to it, Marissa. Enjoy the perfume and rest of your work day," he said as he backed away and turned to leave.

She and the women at the makeup and perfume counters all watched as he walked out of the store. Once he left, all the women from the other counters came over to her to dish about the night to come.

His work day ended at 5:00 p.m., and she rushed home to get ready for her date. Despite the flattery, she said, she told herself to just enjoy a night out and to not take this too seriously. She had never been to Fiona Rose, but she had heard of it and knew that it was a pricey restaurant. To make sure she made a good impression on Tyson and the restaurant, she wore a very elegant, maroon, off-shoulder, fishtail-style dress, with heels to match and a sequined purse to accent the look.

When Marissa arrived at Fiona Rose, she was taken aback at the elegance of the restaurant. The sounds of soothing classical violin filled the air as the hostess escorted her to the table where Tyson was waiting in a nicely tailored black suit.

"You look amazing, Marissa," he said as she took her seat.

She described the night as absolutely wonderful. Tyson was charming, smart, and polite—a perfect gentleman. He could talk about practically any subject that came up during the conversation, which really impressed her. As the night went on and a few glasses of wine were enjoyed, they discussed sports, travel, careers, and goals. He told her that he had recently gotten into the import and export industries. The work paid well, he said, but sometimes required heavy travel. She went on to tell him that she had just relocated to Washington, D.C., from Bridgeport, Connecticut, to start over after her father passed away. He told her that he could relate; he had lost an uncle who raised him after his father left his mother when he was a baby.

The night ended after they finished two lobster tails, steamed mussels, coleslaw, and more wine. He escorted her to her car and asked her if she would see him again this weekend. She agreed, and they exchanged numbers. The follow-up date turned into another date; that date was followed by another date. Before long, Marissa said that she was seeing Tyson regularly and that a relationship had blossomed. She began meeting his friends and taking weekend trips with him. On one particular trip, Marissa said that he was going to Philadelphia for the weekend to secure a deal with a company to ship all their products to Florida. She thought it strange he would be working on a business deal on the weekend, but he told her the client needed to meet today because he was working on other business the following Monday. Marissa didn't want to be a distraction on the trip, but after some convincing, she went with him. He picked her up at about 5:00 p.m., and they headed north.

During the ride to Philadelphia, Tyson told Marissa that he needed to stop in Baltimore first to tie up a loose end. They took an off-ramp and pulled into the parking lot of a diner near Baltimore/Washington International Airport. They parked on the side of the diner.

"I need to make a call, baby," he said as he stepped out of the car.

She said he was trying to talk in a low tone, but she managed to hear him say something along the lines of having arrived and what sounded like a brief description of the car they were in.

He went to her side of the car and said, "I'll be right back, baby," and kissed her on the cheek.

When he turned the corner of the diner, she said she felt uneasiness come over her. Just as she thought to open the car door to exit, a large man opened the car door and held her arms. She said she remembered letting out a scream before seeing another man enter the driver door and place a white cloth over her face. The next thing she said she remembered was waking up on a small plane as it was going down the runway. Next to her was the large man who had opened Tyson's car door. She described the plane as having propellers and not being very big, so the large man sitting next to her seemed to take up most of the space.

"Where are we going, and where's Tyson?" she asked.

He didn't say anything, but his cold stare and facial expression told her everything she needed to know. She was in trouble and didn't need to say another word. Behind her was another man. Not a large man like the one next to her, but it was clear from the way that he looked and talked that he was in control of everything going on. He wouldn't speak directly to her but instead relayed messages through the large man sitting next to her. The man in the back would lean forward, say something to the man next to her in another language, and then the man next to her would ask her if she was thirsty or hungry. What felt like a few hours passed before she felt the plane begin to descend.

The pilot landed the plane at a small airport in what she now realized was somewhere in Florida.

"Get out and don't say anything. You only speak when spoken to," said the man in the back.

They got off the plane and walked toward a white cargo van.

"Get in," said the large man who had been sitting next to her on the plane.

As she looked inside, there were three other young women in the van. All three looked afraid, but one was sobbing uncontrollably. The large man stepped into the van very aggressively. Marissa recalled that she could see the entire van rock and lower several inches when he stepped into it and grabbed the crying woman forcefully by her shoulders.

His voice was reminiscent of a roar as he commanded, "Shut up! Shut up! Stop your crying!"

The woman then said, "I don't want to be here! Please let me go! I have a son back home! I won't say anything if you let me go! Please!"

Before she could continue to plead for her release, the large man smacked her so hard she went unconscious. The man from the back of the plane began cursing at the large man for hitting her.

"Who's going to want to pay for damaged merchandise, you stupid ox?" he yelled.

Marissa knew from the moment she woke up on the plane that she was in trouble, but hearing the man from the plane ask that question made it clear to her that she had indeed been trafficked. The shock of seeing the woman hit so hard made her climb into the van without saying a word.

"You'll have to excuse my heavy-handed friend. He's not as reasonable as I am. You're almost at the end of your journey with us, so if you just ride quietly, there'll be no problems. To make sure you do this for me, my friend will be riding with us."

He then walked over to the pilots, handed them two envelopes, returned to the van, and started it. The large man then shut the van doors, and they left the airstrip. The two conscious women both looked at her as they rode in the back of the van. Marissa said it was as if they were hoping that she had some plan, like they were expecting her to somehow instill hope in them. The truth of the matter, she said, was that she was just as hopeless as they were.

About thirty minutes passed before they arrived at their destination, which was as she described, a palatial house. After parking in the back of the estate, the large man opened the rear doors of the van and told them to get out. He escorted them into what looked like a large, upscale bathroom with multiple showers. The bathroom was connected to a big room full of women's clothing.

"Take a shower and get dressed in something nice. There are people here to see you, so make sure you look your best." After a few awkward moments, the man said to them, "I'm not leaving. Take off your clothes and shower *now!*"

She said that they quickly disrobed and showered with the man watching. The fear as he stoically watched them shower was nearly unbearable. After they showered, he assisted in finding dresses that fit each of them. All the dresses and gowns were fitted and elegant. Once the clothes were chosen, the women were led into a dark room where a light from the back of the room was shining on them. Marissa said she could make out silhouettes of people sitting in the room, but she could not decipher any faces.

The voice of a sophisticated-sounding man came over a sound system.

"Thank you for joining us this evening. The bidding will start momentarily."

The fear Marissa had been gripped by for the last couple of hours was at that moment replaced with embarrassment and anger. The fact that she was being bid on like a steer at a cattle auction infuriated her while simultaneously causing her to experience shame draping over her like a wet wool blanket.

She was joined by the two conscious women from the van and about ten to twelve other women from other rooms in the building. Marissa said that a woman was bid on by several different people in the dark room. Once the bidding for one woman concluded, that woman would be taken to the back of the room, and the auctioneer told the bidder that he could pay in the back and that his purchase would be waiting for him in the collection area.

A million thoughts rushed through her mind, none of which provided an idea for how she could escape being bid on like a piece of property. Her turn came to be auctioned off. She stood emotionless as a man took her by the hand and paraded her around to be viewed. He discussed her ethnicity, physical features, measurements, hair color, eye color, age, height, and weight. She became sad while she was being described on stage in front of a room of strangers because she realized that much of the information given from that point on could not have been learned by the men who took her to that location. Information like her favorite foods, place of origin, and other information had to have been given them by someone who knew her—someone like a boyfriend, someone like Tyson. Despair set in as she realized that the care and adoration he had displayed for her was an act and that everything that he had told her was a lie—a huge charade designed to get her to lower her guard and become an easy target to be snatched away from the life she knew. She said she told herself to remain positive and watchful, but it became increasingly difficult as each moment passed.

Once the bidding was over, she described being taken down a long, dimly lit hallway that led to a large enclosed area that she described as a warehouse with a lot of different cars and vans in it. This was where she first encountered the three men who were just arrested for holding her captive. She told us that her dad always warned her to be aware of her surroundings and take mental notes of everything and everyone she encountered, so despite being terrified, she kept as watchful as possible. She said she noticed that these three men did not display the same type of organization or sophistication as the men from the plane; they often appeared confused about their next step. They also argued among themselves quite a bit, which confirmed her suspicions about them being new to kidnapping. Marissa had heard of human trafficking in the past but didn't think about it too much. After putting what she had heard about it together with what she had observed over the past several hours, she concluded that the men she was now with were buyers. They probably only connected with the men from the plane when they were looking to purchase someone. Their lack of sophistication told her she would probably have a moment to escape if she took her father's advice and paid attention. So that's what she did. Marissa paid attention and looked for any opportunity she could take to either make a break for it or signal for help.

They arrived at the motel next to Kreemy Kone's rather late, so they decided to rest for the night before making her work. Evidently, they told her that a lot of money had been spent to get her here, and it was her job to make that money back for them.

"Make it back how?" she asked.

"You know what it is, girl. Use what your momma gave you. Someone as sexy as you won't have no problem makin' dat money. You start tomorrow. Trying to leave ain't a good idea either," said one of her captors. "Wherever you go, we're watching. As long as you bring back $1,500 or more a day, we good."

After that, they told her that one of them would be outside to make sure she didn't leave. They closed the door behind them and left.

Marissa told us she fought the urge to cry but couldn't help herself. About an hour passed before she could bring herself to peek out of the curtains to see if they were watching her like they said they would. Indeed, one of the men was sitting in the parking space in front of the motel room.

She laid back on the bed and cried herself to sleep, thinking about the horror of selling her body to strangers in order to survive.

A few hours later, Marissa heard the door being keyed open.

"Here are some clothes that are a little more comfortable. Clean yourself up and put these on. We'll be outside," the captor said while throwing a bag of clothes to her.

From the looks of how the sun came in through the window, she guessed that it was about 10:00 a.m. Reluctantly, she began to look through the clothes that were given her. She also saw toothpaste and a toothbrush in the bag, so she brushed her teeth while staring sadly at the person in the mirror who stared sadly back. With a myriad of thoughts running through her mind as to how she got into her present situation, she rinsed her mouth out, took off her clothes, and slowly climbed into the shower. As the sadness crept over her and she began to accept her reality, she couldn't help but think about her father and the fact that he lost his life trying to make sure that she was taken care of. Marissa said she didn't know how she would do it, but it was in that moment she made up her mind that this wasn't going to be her reality.

After finishing her shower, she said she began to stall in the motel room to give herself time to think of what to do to escape. When her captors became irritated and impatient, she came out of the motel. They told her that the area near the motel was where she would run into men who wanted what she had to offer, so they told her to hang out there and make herself available. She said she walked the strip in front of the motel, doing her best to appear as though she was talking to men and striking out. She would merely speak to men walking by and hope that none of them took any interest in her. When someone did take an interest in her, she would blow him off.

When her captors realized what she was doing, they took her back into the motel room and told her they knew what she what she was doing.

"No one has been interested in me," she recalled telling them in a trembling voice.

One of the men then pulled out a straight razor and said, "Bitch, I know what you're doing, and things are going to get pretty damn messy if you keep running guys off. Go get my money! Do you hear me?"

Holding back tears, Marissa nodded, and they sent her back out. She started to go back to the strip in front of the hotel when she looked to her right and saw me ordering ice cream at Kreemy Kone's.

"So what made you approach Alex?" Glen asked.

"I don't know," Marissa responded. "I knew I needed to talk to someone to avoid having those guys hurt me, and something about him looked safe. Like he wouldn't hurt me even if I had to…"

"You don't have to worry about that now," I said.

"I could just tell you were a good man. I was so glad when you asked me if I was in trouble. I was so scared," she said as tears began to roll down her face again.

"So what do we do now, Glen?"

"We have her statement, which is enough to put these three away for a while. We've been hearing about this kind of thing moving into Patrician but haven't been able to get much of a pulse on it. Hopefully these guys can lead us to the bigger players in this game. Miss Johnson, you're free to go. If you like, I can arrange for you to stay at the station if that'll help. Do you have a way to get home?"

"Well, my purse was left in Tyson's car. He didn't know any of my PINs, so I should still have money. I just need to get replacement cards. I'm not going back to D.C. though. I'm going to take some time to figure out my next step."

"Where will you stay, Miss Johnson?" Glen asked.

"I've already paid for the room. She can stay here at least for tonight and gather herself if she likes."

"I think I'd rather do that if you all don't mind. I think I could use the time alone."

"Would you mind if we checked on you tomorrow?" Glen asked.

"No, I'd like that," she said.

"We'll stop by sometime midmorning. Here's $40 so you can order some food from the kitchen tonight," I said.

Glen handed Marissa one of his cards, and she walked us to the door. As she saw us out, she told us again how thankful she was for our help. She hugged us and closed the door behind us. Glen and I agreed to meet the next morning at 9:00 a.m.

"Let's hope tomorrow morning doesn't have another Alex Archer surprise attached to it," Glen said as he got into his squad car and drove off.

The walk back to my car was an interesting one. Although the moment had passed, my mind was going a mile a minute. I'd spent the last twenty years of my life traveling the world, visiting cities and towns in different countries, but I had to return to Patrician to encounter a carjacker and a human trafficker. I knew that Glen was joking, but it was kind of sobering to think that all this had taken place in just two days. I would think that someone with my life experience would have known more about human trafficking, but the reality was, I only thought about something like that if I heard it on the news or saw an article about it online. On one hand, I was glad I didn't know much about it. After all, it's not like kidnapping young women and making them become prostitutes is a subject that your everyday person sits around and discusses over breakfast. On the other hand, I felt bad about not knowing about it. I don't walk around like Bruce Wayne thinking I have the responsibility to drive around in my Batmobile and rid my city of crime, but I couldn't get this one thought out of my mind: *What if I hadn't been there? What could Marissa possibly be forced to endure at this very moment had I not had a desire to run over to Kreemy Kone's and get a double-dipped ice-cream cone?*

When I got to the Mustang, I peeled out of the parking lot and hit the highway to clear my head. Before I knew it, I was nearing Tampa. I spent about an hour at Clearwater Beach just staring at the water, still trying to give my mind a much-needed break from what I had just encountered. Regardless of how hard I tried, I couldn't get the events of the day to stop replaying over and over again in my mind. It took a lot of tossing and turning before I fell asleep that night.

CHAPTER 5

The alarm went off at 8:00 a.m. I must have gotten enough sleep because I didn't have the urge to throw the alarm clock across the room when it sounded. I had a big day ahead, but my excitement about meeting Jack Parker and talking with him about flying the routes to the Tranquil Islands was conflicting with my concern for Marissa. The inner struggle that I was experiencing was suddenly put on pause by a very familiar sound and smell. Few things sounded better to me than faintly hearing my mother and father talking over the sound of utensils and dishes clanking in the morning. That sound always meant that an absolutely amazing breakfast was being prepared. I immediately jumped out of bed and went to the bathroom to brush my teeth and shower. After showering, I went back to my bedroom to pick out something to wear to my meeting with Jack Parker. I wanted to make a good impression, but I also didn't want to melt from wearing a suit and tie on a summer day in Florida. I picked out a pair of khaki dress slacks, a white Ralph Lauren polo shirt, and brown Ralph Lauren shoes. I grabbed a pair of shades and my Breitling and headed downstairs. About halfway down the staircase, I was met by the aroma of freshly cooked scrambled eggs, turkey bacon, and coffee that quickly made my stomach start to growl.

"I see not much has changed," I heard Mom say as I stepped off the last stair.

"What do you mean, Mama?"

"You always came running when you smelled food cooking."

"Looking good, son," Dad said. "Where are you headed all jazzed up this morning?"

"I'm meeting with one of the owners of Patrician Gulf Charters. They fly short flights from here to the Bahamas and the Tranquil Islands. They had a couple of pilots move on recently, and they need to find someone to pick up those routes. The owners have had to fly those routes the pilots left, so they're going to be eager to hire someone qualified to fly. Gonna do some house hunting as well after I talk to them."

"Sounds like you're going to be back in the air soon."

"Let's hope so, but in the meantime, I'm going to dive into this breakfast!"

I ate breakfast and enjoyed talking with Mom and Dad but was mindful to not mention what happened with Marissa. Hearing yesterday's events would have sent Mom over the moon. It would probably send Dad over right behind her, but he wouldn't show it nearly as much. I got a text from Glen telling me that he was heading to the hotel. I finished my coffee, kissed Mom on the cheek, and headed over to the hotel with the top down on the Mustang.

I pulled up to the hotel at about 8:45 a.m. and walked into the hotel lobby. A few minutes later, Glen parked his squad car in front of my Mustang and met me inside. From the time we were teammates in high school, Glen had a very confident air about him, never cocky, just very confident in who he was and what he could do. We won state championships in the 4x100 relay and never lost a race in the event, all season. He was third leg, and I ran anchor. He relished the fact that he was the only White guy on a state championship level relay. Regardless of how tough our opponents were rumored to be, I always felt our confidence bolster when Glen would walk up to me and say, "You know I'm gonna give you the baton with a good lead, don't you?" before shaking my hand and jogging over to the second exchange zone on the track. He never failed to deliver, and that confident jog down to the finish line to celebrate with me, Allen, and Jerome Roberts was the icing on the cake. This morning was different, however. Something was a little different about Glen when he walked into the hotel lobby to meet me. The confidence that always showed up in his walk was still there, but the look on his face told another story. That cool demeanor was not present in his eyes, regardless of how hard he tried to make it appear so. Glen was nervous, and it showed.

"You all right, man?" I asked.

"I don't know, Arch. I don't think I should have let her stay here alone. I should have insisted she stay at the station or left a female officer with her. I hardly slept thinking about it, man."

"I'm sure she's all right Glen. Let's just go up and make sure."

Just like the day before, we rode the elevator back up to the fifteenth floor where Marissa was staying.

"Good morning, Marissa. This is Officer Hixon with Patrician PD," Glen announced while knocking on the door. The stillness and silence on the other side of the door was deafening. With a concerned frown on his brow, Glen knocked again and repeated, "Good morning, Marissa. This is Officer Hixon with Patrician PD."

Nothing. Just as I was about to knock, Glen and I heard the elevator stopping on our floor. We both turned toward it, desperately wanting to see Marissa step out of it, but instead, our hopes were dashed when a housekeeper stepped out instead.

With a puzzled look on her face, likely caused by her being the focal point of our disappointed gaze, she asked, "Can I help you guys with something?"

"Yes, ma'am. We're here to see the person staying in this room. Would you please open the door for us so we can make sure she is okay?" Glen asked.

"Sure. No problem," she answered as she began to calmly rifle through items on her cleaning cart to find the keys. She finally located the key to the room and opened the door.

"Marissa… Marissa?" we inquired upon entering the room.

Our disappointment quickly shifted to concern as we got no response. We checked the bathroom and found no one. The bed appeared to have been slept in, or at least laid on for a while, but Marissa was nowhere to be found.

"Check your phone, Glen, to see if she called or texted you," I said.

"Nothing from her at all," Glen replied while scrolling through his text messages.

I turned to the housekeeper and asked, "Have you seen the woman who stayed here last night?"

"No, sir, I haven't. I just got to work about fifteen minutes ago," she said.

"Let's go back downstairs. Maybe she decided to get breakfast. Hopefully she didn't just check out and leave without saying goodbye," I said.

We thanked the housekeeper and headed back downstairs. We searched the lobby, the hotel restaurant, the pool, gym, and anywhere we could think of. We finally thought to ask the front-desk lady if Marissa had checked out or if she had seen her.

"She didn't check out. She walked out the front door and went to the right."

"Was she with someone?" Glen asked.

"I didn't see her with anyone, but she did turn and look, like someone called her name."

"What do you mean?"

"Exactly what I said. She turned like someone called her name."

"Did she say she knew anyone here, Arch?"

"No, she didn't."

Glen turned back to the desk lady and asked, "How did she look when she turned to the right? Did she look happy to see the person? Was she scared? Surprised?"

"Neither. You know the look that someone gives a person when they're familiar with them but not really friends with them? That's how she looked."

"How long ago was this?" Glen asked.

"Fifteen, maybe twenty minutes at the most."

We thanked her and sat in the lobby to see if she would return. After about an hour of waiting and catching up with Glen, I got a phone call.

"Mr. Archer, this is Jack Parker with Patrician Gulf Charters. We came back early from the Tranquils. Is now a bad time for you to come and take a look around the airstrip?'

"Not at all. I was just catching up with an old friend."

"Friends are important, Mr. Archer, and I'm about an hour and a half early in calling, so if you want to wait about an hour to finish catching up..."

"Oh, this guy? He's not that important. He's actually a pain in the ass, Mr. Parker, so I'll be over shortly," I said with a laugh while watching Glen silently mouth, "Kiss my White ass."

"Great! Edward has said a lot of good things about you, Mr. Archer, so I look forward to meeting you."

"I look forward to meeting you as well. See you soon."

"Gotta run, Glen."

"Cool. What's that about?"

"Meeting with the owners of a charter company. They may want me to start flying for them. Let me know if Marissa turns up."

"I will, man. Good luck with your meeting. Let me know how it goes."

"Will do."

I trotted over to the Mustang and hopped in. When I got seated and strapped in, I paused a minute after starting my car to look around, hoping to catch a glimpse of Marissa walking up. I was in great spirits about my upcoming meeting with Mr. Parker, but I couldn't get past what the front-desk lady said about Marissa, that Marissa had turned and looked as though someone called her name. Other than the guys who trafficked her, who would know her here? Who knows? Maybe I just got played for a night in a nice hotel, but I can't get ignore what I saw in her eyes. I know trouble when I see it—and I saw trouble. Nevertheless, duty called, and I had to focus, so I cleared my mind and headed to Patrician Gulf Charters. I hoped that the drive to the airstrip would clear my head of the situation with Marissa, but I couldn't help but feel that something was wrong; my inability to put my finger on it was weighing on me like a ship's anchor.

As I drove past Edward's housing development, I noted how much this area had evolved since I had left Patrician. This area used to be nothing but scattered forest, fields, and beaches that no one wanted to visit because of how far away it used to seem. The landscape was nice but kind of desolate back then. I used to hear about the stoner kids going out here to get high. That had never been my thing, so I never had any reason to venture out this far. Seeing the new houses and shopping plazas in a part of the city that was once referred to as "way out in the country" reminded me that I was not in the same Patrician I had left over two decades ago.

Outside the newer criminal activity I had just encountered, the changes I had seen so far had been good.

I came around a bend and caught my first glimpse of the airstrip. As a pilot, I have seen more airstrips than I can count, but I can safely say that this one impressed me. It may have been because of the low expectations I had based on the repeated references to the location as an airstrip. Calling this a mere airstrip was like calling the Hope Diamond a rock. This was more like a miniature airport. Airstrips tend to only have planes, hangars to house the planes, and runways. This "airstrip" had everything. There were small terminals, shuttle carts used to take people to the planes they were flying out on, state-of-the art air traffic control tower, restaurants, gift shops, a car rental station, and even a small hotel. What stood out to me the most, aside from all that, was the number of people I saw and the number of planes. When I hear "airstrip," a basic place used to train pilots comes to mind. Outside of seeing pilots learning to fly, one may see a few select businessmen fortunate enough to own and house a plane preparing to fly out. Nothing at all like this. The airport was gated and staffed with security that you first met at the guard shack in the front of the airport. The signs on both sides of the guard shack read, "Welcome to Patrician Gulf Airport."

It seems that Patrician Gulf Airport and Edward's homeowners' association go to the same company in search of security guards because I drove up to the guard shack and was met by another large, stoic security guard packing a Glock 19 on his hip.

"I'm here to see Jack Parker," I said.

"You must be Mr. Archer. Mr. Parker and his party are in the offices inside Hangar 3. I'll tell them you're on the way."

"Thank you."

I drove about a quarter mile, turned right at the hangars, and parked in front of Hangar 3. The row of hangars went on for quite a bit past Hangar 3. As I pulled in front of the hangar, I saw people begin to move around in an office at the back of the hangar.

The door to the office opened, and Edward stuck his head out and said, "Go ahead and pull your car inside in front of the plane on the right. We're in here waiting for you."

I gave him a thumbs-up and pulled up in front of the plane he directed me to. I parked, hopped out, and began walking toward the office. The hangar held four beautifully shined-up turboprops, two Beechcraft King Air 350s, and two 350 ERS. One of the 350 ERS was having routine maintenance done, so I spoke to the aircraft mechanic as I neared the office door. I walked into the office to a chorus of greetings.

"Mr. Archer, I'm Jack Parker, and it's a pleasure to meet you."

"The pleasure's mine, sir."

"You already know Edward. The man to his left is my brother, James."

"Pleasure to meet you as well, Mr. Parker."

"No need for formalities, Alex. Just call me James. So what do you think about the airstrip?"

"I think calling it an airstrip is a bit of an understatement. This is extremely nice."

"I hear that all the time. Jack and Edward tell me that you flew the KC-135 in the Air Force. Nice plane. You should be fine in about anything we have in our fleet."

"Absolutely. You carry mostly Beechcraft, or do you have any others? I saw quite a few hangars down the row."

"Oh yeah! We have everything from a Falcon 7X and Gulfstream G700 that we use for international travel to Cessna Stationairs and Piaggio Avantis. Any one of those you not comfortable flying?"

"No. Just put me behind the stick, and I'll make it work."

"Good to hear, Alex! We just had two pilots bail on us, and we're needing to get their routes covered as soon as we can."

"Why did they leave?" I asked.

"Their wives found really good jobs out of town, so they had to become the trailing spouses and follow them," Edward responded.

"Oh, okay. Mind if I see more of the facilities?"

"Not at all. I'll grab a cart, and we can ride around a bit."

James radioed one of the airport attendants to bring a six-seater golf cart to the hangar. We piled onto the cart, and off we went.

Edward and Jack talked among themselves while James pointed out various details about the airport. We drove past the hotel, control tower, gift shops, and terminals before returning to the row of hangars. As a pilot, I was eager to get back to the hangars to see what other planes were there. There were thirty hangars divided into two parallel rows. Each hangar appeared to house planes according to their respective manufacturers; Beechcrafts were with Beechcrafts, Cessnas were with Cessnas, Pipers with Pipers, and so on.

"Do you guys own all of these planes?" I asked.

"Not all of them, but we do own a few. A lot of these are owned by businesses or individuals. Ten are ours, and those are the planes that you'll fly to the Tranquils. We'll talk about the rest over lunch. Sound good?"

"Fine by me."

James leaned forward and said, "Please take us to Burner's Diner."

The driver whipped around, and we headed back toward the front of the airport. It was midday, and all the drama of the morning with not knowing where Marissa was had stirred up my appetite. The aroma that hit us as we entered the restaurant only made the hunger pangs intensify. Burner's Diner had a very nice aviator theme which I appreciated. Model airplanes and jets, ranging from the Wright brothers Flyer to SR-71s and Stealth Bombers, hung from the ceiling. It really did my heart some good to see a few Stratotankers hanging up there. Articles about famous aviation events complemented the theme perfectly. The hostess saw James enter the diner first, followed by the rest of us, and immediately signaled to a waiter to prepare a table. While we waited to be seated, I excused myself to use the restroom and call Glen to see if he had heard anything from Marissa. I got no answer, so I left him a message to call me back. Despite how hard I tried to fix it in my mind that Marissa had simply left on her own accord, I couldn't help but feel that she had stumbled into some more trouble. That feeling sat in the pit of my stomach like an overcooked steak, and I knew it was going to continue to nag me until I found out what happened to her. For the time being, however, I had to manage that feeling so I could handle business and talk money without appearing distracted or disinterested.

I washed my hands and headed toward the dining room. The hostess saw me walking near the bar and directed me to where James, Jack, and Edward were seated.

I reached the table, and James said, "Order whatever you want, Alex. It's on me."

The menu was standard bar-and-grill-type food: burgers, fries, steaks, nachos, and the like. Many of the entrees were named after famous pilots or aviation events to further complement the aviation theme of the restaurant. Edward, James, and Jack all ordered steaks. I'm not much of a steak-eater, so I ordered the Chuck Yeager chicken sandwich.

"Not a red-meat guy, I see," observed Jack.

"No, I'm not. It's not that I don't like it. It just doesn't like me back when I eat it."

"Say no more!" laughed James. "I need to stop eating so much of it myself. So. You've seen what we're working with. What's it gonna take to get you to come fly for us?"

"What's a realistic number of flights you can guarantee me per week?"

"Great question. You'll get no less than two per week and can have more if you want."

"That's fair. So what do you pay per run?"

"Jack and I think that about $1,500 a run is fair."

At that figure, I kept a straight face on the outside, but if you could have seen my emotions, I probably looked like that famous picture of Buckwheat, typically used to illustrate a surprised person. The truth is, I would have been happy with about $1,000 a run.

In negotiation, it's always good to make a counteroffer, but I was honestly so happy about what they offered I asked, "Can you do $1,600?" to avoid looking like a pushover.

"Do we have a deal at $1,600 if we say yes?"

"I think we do," I responded.

"Then, yes, it is! Welcome to the team, Alex! That was easy enough, right?"

We continued to talk and enjoy our meals. Edward ordered a couple of bottles of wine from the bar, and the good times continued.

During the conversation, I asked, "On a weekend that I'm not flying for you all, can I take a plane out and do some flying of my own?"

"What do you mean?" Jack asked with a curious look on his face.

"What I mean is, can I take a plane out for my own use? I have a niece and nephew that are like a son and daughter to me, and I would like to take them out every so often. If it's not okay…"

"It's okay. Just be mindful that you may be required to cover your fuel. I didn't mean to look so suspicious. We had to dismiss a pilot because he began to sneak his own passengers onto under-booked flights and take them to their destination after he flew our passengers to theirs. He would keep whatever money they paid him. I think he was picking up and dropping off drugs too."

With my hands up, I said, "Wow! Well, you don't have to worry about that with me. I'm just trying to maintain my status as the cool uncle for my niece and nephew. The most I would want to do is to take them and maybe a couple friends to the Bahamas or the Tranquils every so often."

"No worries, Alex. Just make sure you use one of the airport's planes. Make sure it isn't scheduled out, and it won't be a problem."

About midway through the second bottle of wine, my phone rang. I looked down and saw that Glen was returning my call. I excused myself to answer his.

"What's up, Arch! I see I missed a call from you."

"Yeah. I was just checking to see if Marissa turned up."

"Nothing yet, and to be honest Arch, it kind of bothers me. Your meeting go okay?"

"Excellent, actually!"

"Good to hear. Let me get back to work, man. I'll keep an eye out for her, and I'll let you know if anything turns up."

"Sounds like a plan. Take it easy, Glen."

"You too, Arch."

I returned to the table with mixed emotions. I was ecstatic about stumbling into such a well-paying gig on one hand; on the other, I was worried sick about a young lady who, before yesterday, I had no clue existed. The day went on, and I continued to enjoy my time with Edward, Jack, and James. We returned to their office, signed papers, and set my schedule for the upcoming week. Everything wrapped up at about 9:30 p.m. I drove out of the airport with a smile on my face but a heaviness in my gut because I couldn't shake my concern for Marissa. Glen hadn't called with any updates, so I couldn't escape the feeling that something was wrong. A great day was followed by a sleepless night.

CHAPTER 6

The week finished without another incident involving me fighting or evading criminals. That was a relief because I was beginning to think I had become some sort of magnet for trouble. The day after signing my paperwork with Patrician Gulf Airport, I stayed in Mom and Dad's house to avoid running into a situation. I wasn't sitting at home afraid to go outside. It just felt good to have some normalcy unfold in my life again. Flying top-secret missions to help our soldiers take the fight to people who wanted to harm America and her allies felt much more normal than fighting carjackers in front of my father and nephew in Patrician. It certainly felt more normal than encountering a potential sex-trafficking victim in Patrician—if indeed that's what she was. The week finishing without any incidents also meant the week finishing without hearing from Marissa. By this time, that feeling in my gut which had me so concerned last week had been replaced with a sort of indifference. It wasn't that I no longer cared about what happened to her. She just was out of sight and therefore had begun to dissipate from my mind. My thoughts of, *God, I pray she's okay*, were slowly replaced with, *I wonder if she's all right*, or *Did I get scammed?*

I think Glen had begun to feel the same way. We met up to hang out several times that week, and I think we mentioned Marissa once or twice. Even those mentions were fleeting, with the entire conversation going along the lines of, "Arch, have you heard from that girl again?"

"Nope. Have you?"

"Nah. You want to grab a beer after I finish my shift?"

She had been relegated to a passing thought, and I honestly was okay with that.

The weekend came, and I was ready to hang out with my niece and nephew. Calvin had spent the entire week taunting Candace about how much he enjoyed hanging out with Uncle Alex and Grandpa and the "action" she missed. She began to feel bothered that I hadn't come to hang out with her yet. So I planned a time for Candace and me to go get ice cream ourselves. I had a little surprise planned, however, something sure to give me more points as the cool uncle; something guaranteed to get Candace and Calvin engaged in harmless bickering in front of Devin about whose Uncle Alex story was the best.

On Friday, I had talked to James about taking a Cessna 205 for the weekend. The plan was to tell Candace that we were going to get some ice cream, knowing that she would assume Kreemy Kone's. I would surprise her by instead taking her to New Smyrna Beach in the Cessna and getting ice cream at the Dairy Queen there. Candace loves being in an airplane and has begged me to take her flying since she was a little girl, so I knew this was going to be a hit.

On Saturday I picked Candace up at about 11:00 a.m. I told Devin and Mike that we would get some ice cream and hang out for a little while so they wouldn't be worried when we didn't come back after about an hour or so. We headed toward the beach where Kreemy Kone's was located.

As we neared it, I said, "I don't want Kreemy Kone's today. I'm gonna take you by this new spot."

She gave me a confused look and asked, "No Kreemy Kone's for you, Uncle Alex? This new place must be good!"

"Trust me. You'll love this. It's by the airport."

"Way out there?" she queried. "This must be some really good ice cream!"

We got to the airport and pulled into the row of hangars. I could see her wheels turning. The eagerness welling up inside of her was beginning to show in her face.

"You're finally going to take me flying, aren't you?" she asked while literally hopping in place.

One of the mechanics had just completed routine maintenance on a particular Cessna 205. I had slipped him a fifty-dollar bill to listen for us as we arrived. At that very moment, he opened up Hangar 18 to unveil the Cessna. The smile on her face as she hugged me and ran to the plane was all the thanks I needed.

She must have circled that plane ten times before I finally asked, "Are you just gonna walk around it and drool, or do you want to take it up with me?"

Without hesitation she opened the door and climbed into the front right seat. Candace and Calvin have flown with their parents to visit me in Washington on numerous occasions, but she always told me that she thought flying with me in a smaller plane would be a lot more fun for her.

I checked a few things out on the plane, fired her up, and we took off.

We were cleared to take off westward. The airport sits next to a private beach owned by James and Jack Parker, which means we would take off over the gulf before changing direction to head east toward New Smyrna Beach on the Atlantic side of Florida. Candace's face lit up like a Christmas tree when I took a hard bank right over the water to head east. I thought it would make her a little nervous, but she just smiled even bigger. The girl's tough. I wouldn't be shocked if she started asking me about flight school.

The flight from Patrician to New Smyrna Beach is about an hour long, so that gave us some time to catch up. She told me about school, her college and career plans, and whatever else popped into her mind. It was a clear and beautiful Florida day in the summer, and listening to Candace talk about everything under the sun made the day even more beautiful. We landed at New Smyrna Municipal Airport about 12:20 p.m. and caught an Uber to the Dairy Queen. I ordered my usual Peanut Buster Parfait, and Candace ordered a Blizzard. We did more of what we had been doing for the past couple of hours, which was to gab and gab some more, before calling another Uber to take us back to the airport. Just as we arrived, Devin called asking how much longer I would have Candace out.

"Not long. Maybe another hour or so. Why?" I asked.

"Nothing major. I was just thinking about getting something to eat soon. I wondered if you wanted to meet Allen and me."

"That sounds like a plan, Devin. Let me finish spoiling my niece, and I'll be there."

"Stop spoiling her, Alex, and what's all that noise? You take her to the airport or something?"

"Yeah, something like that. Listen, gotta go so I can finish showing her around."

"You better not have taken her up in…"

"Sorry, Dev! Connection is bad. I think I'm losing you," I said as I hung up the phone.

On top of being mouthy, my sister, Devin, can be a bit neurotic, and she has always been scared of flying in a smaller plane like a Cessna. I made sure that Mike was okay with me flying Devin around. He just said he would conveniently not be around if Devin found out. We landed back at Patrician Gulf Airport at about 3:20 p.m.

"This was the best day of my life, Uncle Alex! Thank you for finally taking me flying with you."

"The pleasure is mine, sweetheart!"

"I heard you talking to Momma when we were in New Smyrna Beach. You like torturing Momma through us, don't you?" she asked while laughing.

With a sly little smirk, I said, "I don't know what you're talking about," and winked at her.

Before leaving, I took Candace by the office that I report to so she would know where it was in case she or Calvin needed me at the airport. I checked my scheduled flights for the upcoming week and then drove Candace home. On the way home, she talked about how much fun she had in the Cessna. She even began asking about learning to fly at Embry Riddle University, which made my face light up about as bright as her face did when I first took her up.

As we approached Mike and Devin's house, we could see Calvin shooting hoops in the driveway. The closer we got, the bigger the smile on Candace's face became. I could see her wheels spinning about the many different ways she could rub the Cessna trip in her brother's face.

The Mustang hadn't come to a full stop before she was hopping out and running up to Calvin, saying, "*Ha!* Guess what we did!"

I parked the car and walked up to the driveway.

"You're lying, Candace!" I heard Calvin say with a look of shock on his face.

"Uncle Alex! Y'all really went flying in a Cessna?"

I simply responded with a smile. Mike and Devin stepped out on their porch after hearing Candace and Calvin talking in the driveway. I gave Candace a wink as I began to back away toward the Mustang.

"Hey, bro! Thanks for getting my baby back to me. We're about to go shopping. Why are you grinning and backing away?"

I glanced over at Mike, who by this time looked as though he'd just remembered that he'd agreed to let his only daughter do something he knew his wife wouldn't want her to do.

"I forgot something inside, baby," he nervously said to Devin as he trotted back into the house.

She stared curiously at Mike as he walked back inside.

Mentally machinating, she walked over to Candace, who was grinning as big as the Cheshire cat in Wonderland,

and said to her, "You must have had a really good time with your uncle! What else did you guys do?"

Candace glanced at me, who by this time was backing away faster and grinning bigger. The Mustang was still running, so I hopped in and put it in drive with my foot on the brake.

Devin then turned to me and said, "I know that funky-assed grin, Alex! You're up to something! You're always spoiling them! What did you do?"

Candace started giggling and said, "I'm gonna go check on Daddy."

The only two people left in the driveway were perhaps two of the most talkative people on the planet.

I knew that Calvin was going to begin to gush information like a geyser, so I slowly took my foot off of the brake as he spouted, "Ma'! Uncle Alex took Candace flying!"

Once those words left his lips, I hit the gas while laughing out loud. The only thing I could make out as I pulled off was, "I know you didn't take my baby up in one of those little-assed planes, Alex!"

While driving off, I thought about how happy Candace was, how Calvin was going to talk about it all night, and most importantly, that Devin was—and the fact that I earned more points toward being the best uncle on the planet! My job was done.

The start of the week was perfect! On Sunday night, Jack emailed me the schedule for my first week so I could look it over and plan my week accordingly. I made sure I got a good night's rest to be refreshed and ready to go on Monday morning. James told me doubles were rare, but my first day on the job was a double run. I had a family that was eager to vacation on the Tranquil Islands for the week, so they scheduled their departure time for 8:30 a.m. I would have a few hours to kill before I picked up another family and flew them to the Orlando. I was a little excited about this flight because, despite how much I'd traveled in my career as a pilot, I'd never been to the Tranquil Islands. As a kid, I had heard of them, but back then, I never really thought about going. To a Black kid in East Patrician, the Tranquil Islands was that destination "way out there" where the rich White folks went. I'd hear affluent kids at school talk about visiting the islands with their parents over the weekend, but I'd never thought about them much more than that. From what I gathered back then, it was a high-end place rich people went to so they could party with other rich people and do whatever it was rich people did. When I sat back and thought about it during the weekend, the Tranquil Islands almost had an air of secrecy about them. People talked about them, but there always seemed to be a rush to change the subject for some reason. I never really cared to hear about the islands because in my mind I had what I needed in my neighborhood, and it always seemed weird that people wanted to rush past the topic when the Tranquil Islands were mentioned.

With my curiosity piqued, I arrived at the airport at 6:30 a.m. I do intermittent fasting as a rule; my last meal was at around 4:00 p.m. yesterday, so I was starving. I ran into Burner's Diner and ordered a fried egg sandwich on a croissant with mozzarella cheese and turkey bacon and a coffee. I was delighted when my breakfast sandwich arrived.

This thing was massive, and judging by the look on my server's face when she placed it on my table, my eagerness to dive into it was apparent. I devoured that sandwich like there was no tomorrow; I finished it in about ten minutes. You know you're hungry when you begin to talk about your food despite the fact that no one is sitting there with you. I kept saying, "Aw, man! This is great!" while licking my fingers after every two or three bites. Thankfully, Burner's didn't have a lot of patrons at the time to watch me eat like a man who's been lost at sea for a week.

"That sandwich didn't stand a chance, did it?" said my waitress. "Did you even taste it?" She chuckled.

I took a sip of coffee, wiped my mouth, and said, "Taste what?" with a laugh.

"Good to see you have a sense of humor, fly-boy. My name's Julia. I'm here most mornings. What's your name?"

"I'm Alex. Alex Archer."

"Oh! I heard Jack and James talking about you in here yesterday. They're really glad to have you flying for them. Well, Alex, I have to get back to the kitchen. Just ask for me when you come in, and I'll make sure you're taken care of."

"Will do, Julia. Thank you. Oh…may I have a coffee to go please?"

"You got it, fly-boy. Be safe today."

I took my coffee and headed to Hangar 19 where the Piaggio Avantis were housed. Outside of a Stratotanker, this is probably one of my favorite planes. I love its look with the forewings near the nose of the plane and its turbo-props fixed in a pusher configuration. Gives it a style that sets it apart from other planes in its class. I got to the hangar expecting to see nothing but Avanti P180s, but there were two new Avanti EVOs that were calling my name. I looked at the flight itinerary for the two EVOs, and sure enough, my name along with the Wellington family name was next to one of them. I went through my checklist to make sure everything was ready for takeoff and then waited for 8:30 a.m. to arrive. There were a few magazines about real estate and financial investing in the hangar office, so I had a lot to read until the Wellingtons arrived. My second flight was a pick-up on the Tranquils that I had to drop off at Orlando International Airport. That flight wouldn't leave until noon, so I'd have a few hours to look around after we landed.

At about 7:50, Jack pulled up in his new Mercedes Benz SL 55.

"Hey-hey, Alex! Good to see you, buddy! Just thought I'd come out for your first flight for us. You need anything?"

"Thanks, Jack! I really appreciate that! Nothing that I can think of right now. I'm good to go. I have the Wellington family this morning. Anything I should know about them?"

"Not really. Other than the husband being a neurosurgeon and the wife being a real estate broker, I don't know too much about them. Edward knows the wife pretty well because they're both in the same field. I've talked to them a few times casually, and they seem to be pretty nice."

"Great! I need to talk to someone about buying a house, so she's definitely someone I want to check out."

No later than that, a call came across the radio announcing that the Wellingtons were in the main terminal, preparing to walk down Concourse B to the runway. They were a bit early, so I told Jack I'd catch up with him later. I jumped in the Evo, fired it up, and headed toward Concourse B. As I pulled up, I saw the Wellingtons standing outside. Looking at the two of them, I wasn't sure if I was looking at a real-life couple or at a walking advertisement for a high-end couture clothing line. It was almost surreal to watch them walk toward the plane: the husband with his perfectly styled and trimmed blonde hair, sunglasses perched atop his head, polo shirt, sweater draped across his shoulders, khaki shorts, and Dr. Martens shoes; the wife with her shoulder-length blond hair blowing in the wind, sundress, sandals, and Louis Vuitton purse.

"Ken Wellington," he said as he confidently walked to me and extended his hand.

I shook his hand and introduced myself, adding that I was happy to be flying them to their destination this morning. He stood slightly taller than I, around six feet and four inches, with clear blue eyes. He had a squared jawline and lean, muscular physique, indicative of a man who kept himself fit.

He waved his hand toward his wife and said, "This is my lovely wife, Marjorie."

The look on his face as he introduced Marjorie told everyone that he knew wherever he went with her, he was sure he had the best-looking woman in the room with him; looking at her, she knew it too. Can't say I disagreed with them either. Regardless of whether a man was into blonds or not, this woman was going to turn a man's head in her direction whenever she walked by. Five feet and nine inches or so, a build like a fitness instructor, suntanned skin, and perfect proportions. You could tell she was very well trained in using her hazel-green eyes to tantalize, to have a person eating out of the palm of her hand.

I pulled myself out of her gaze, steadied my professional tone internally before speaking, and said, "Pleasure to meet you both. Just the two of you, I presume?"

"No, we have three more coming," said Marjorie. "Our two adopted children and our housekeeper." She then turned to Ken and asked, "Would you please go in and see what's keeping them?"

Ken nodded and began to walk toward the door to Concourse B. The door opened once Ken got about halfway to it, and out walked two elementary school-aged kids: a boy and a girl. Accompanying them was a Black woman with braids that reached the middle of her back. She stood about five feet and nine inches and had smooth dark skin, high cheekbones, and light-brown eyes. If I had to guess, I would say she was around thirty years old. The children excitedly ran toward Ken, who squatted down and picked them up in his arms. While holding them, he kissed them on their cheeks and placed them back down on the tarmac to go to Marjorie. He waited on the other woman to get to him after putting his children down. When she got closer, he leaned down to her and whispered something in her ear she appeared to have to adhere to regardless of whether she wanted to or not. She walked toward the plane, trying her best to look as though nothing was wrong, but it was to no avail. She was clearly bothered by something. The Wellingtons had several bags with them that this woman knew were her responsibility to load onto the plane. As they walked toward the plane, I walked to the grouping of luggage to assist her in loading them into the cargo bay of the plane.

"It's okay, sir. I got it. Just open the baggage compartment please," she said.

Judging from her accent, I guessed she was from a West African country, possibly Nigeria or Cameroon. Despite performing a task she didn't want to do, she did so with a regality that seemed to drape upon her shoulders like a cloak. She held her head high as she loaded the bags one by one and evenly placed them in the baggage compartment. Once the bags were loaded, she sat down in a seat and quietly strapped herself in. As soon as the Wellingtons were all strapped in, I taxied the runway and waited for clearance by the tower for departure. Ken and Marjorie talked among themselves about the late breakfast they were going to have once we landed on the island while the children anxiously awaited takeoff. Once cleared, we powered down the runway and took off. We quickly climbed to about twenty thousand feet to avoid some turbulence I felt shortly after takeoff. Once at that altitude, I leveled off, and everything was smooth.

While in the air, I again thought about how strange it was I had never gone to these islands that I was now about to frequent. Despite having never visited them, I knew about the rich history of the Tranquil Islands. They are a grouping of three islands about a hundred or so miles off the southern Gulf Coast of Florida. If you go by the history books, the Tranquil Islands were discovered by the Spanish conquistador, Ponce de Leon, on his second voyage to Florida. What the history books don't go into is that when de Leon landed on the main island, he found it was inhabited by Seminole Indians and escaped African slaves who wanted no part of what they saw coming from European colonialism. Traditional history tells us that de Leon and his party stopped at the Tranquil Islands, saw nothing of interest, and left; the truth was that they were run off by the Seminoles and escaped Africans. No one knows exactly what became of the inhabitants, but over the next three hundred years, the islands remained uninhabited. Legend has it that many of those people returned to the mainland, and those who remained simply died off. Regardless of what happened, the legend of the Seminoles and escaped African slaves who teamed up to fight colonialism lives on to this very day. After they were gone, the islands stayed uninhabited for a while until wealthy men began to use them as a weekend getaway to take their mistresses. They started off just parking their yachts off the coast, but before long, things changed on the Tranquil Islands.

No one is certain what year it happened, but most agree that the Tranquil Islands started to become a hot spot in the 1960s. Before the US tourism embargo which President Kennedy placed on it in 1962/1963, Cuba was a place where wealthy Floridians (mostly on the Atlantic side of the state) traveled and partied on the weekends. After the embargo, those same wealthy Floridians, still in need of a weekend spot, started going to the Tranquils. There wasn't much to see at first, but that all changed once the right people saw opportunity. It's uncertain who first purchased them, but the islands were bought outright and construction began shortly after. The fact that the islands were privately owned meant that the general public no longer had access to them. Before long, everything from hotels, restaurants, golf courses, and theme parks were being built on the main island. Soon after, a small airport was erected so people could have more than sailing in as an option. Other than having a few residents, not much was going on with the other two islands from what I hear. They both sit about ten miles from the main island named St. Cesare. St. Dante is an extinct volcano that sits ten miles to the south of St. Cesare, and St. Cecil is the third island that sits about ten miles to the west. After a few years of construction, the Tranquil Islands became the place to go if you had the money to go there.

As I approached them, I was surprised to see how developed St. Cesare was. I expected to see a few hotels and maybe the amusement park I had heard of, but I could see much more as the distance between the island and me grew shorter. The island was a lot larger than I had expected, and there were a lot more buildings I could see in the distance. Instead of having the feel of a tranquil and peaceful resort, part of St. Cesare had a very metropolitan look and feel from the air. It was definitely impressive.

I landed the plane and was directed to the main concourse on the north side of the airport. I shut down the engines, thanked the Wellingtons and their children's caretaker for flying with me, and I assisted them with arrival. The Wellingtons deplaned while their nanny unloaded their baggage.

"Do you have to fly back to Patrician immediately?" asked Marjorie.

"No. I have a few hours before I have to take a couple of guys to Orlando International Airport."

"Good! So you can have breakfast with us."

I didn't particularly care to have breakfast with them. I wasn't hungry for one thing, and secondly, I didn't really like the air about these people. Despite all the warmth they tried to project by doting on their two adopted children, something just felt off about them, so much so I decided to not ask her about purchasing a house.

To avoid appearing rude, I put a big smile on my face and said, "Wow! Thanks for the offer, Marjorie, but I ate at Burner's Diner before takeoff."

"Oh, stop it!" she said in a seemingly jovial tone. "You know you don't want to just sit at this airport for the next couple of hours. Just come hang out with us. It would be good to get to know each other, as I'm sure we'll be flying with you again sometime soon."

The more she talked, I couldn't help but be reminded of a passage from the Bible that my mother used to quote me in high school before I went on dates: *For the lips of a strange (immoral) woman drip honey, and her mouth is smoother than oil.*

She wasn't going to take no for an answer, and any further refusal on my part was going to become awkward, so I said, "Sure, but on one condition. You guys have to show me around the island a little bit. It looks like there's a lot more to this island than I thought there was."

"Oh, you have no idea!"

We walked into the concourse and headed to the car rental counter. Ken didn't even make it to the counter before the attendant said, "Mr. Wellington, we have your usual waiting."

Parked outside was a new cream-colored Cadillac Escalade. As the Wellingtons walked toward the Escalade, I went to assist their nanny with the bags she had loaded onto a baggage cart.

"Don't worry about that, Alex. She's got it."

Reluctantly, I proceeded to the Escalade and left her to load the bags on her own. We piled into the Escalade and left the airport. As we drove toward the city part of the island, I noticed the golf courses and mansions dotting the countryside. There were also a lot of ranches with cattle and horses. As we entered the city, I was surprised by the hustle and bustle. This place was a rather-thriving metropolis in the middle of the gulf. There were banks, auto dealerships, grocery stores, shopping malls, high-rise hotels, restaurants, dance clubs, and many other things that make up a thriving city. It was midmorning, and this place was bustling.

I was sitting in the middle captain's chair on the passenger side, so I leaned forward and asked, "How many people live here?"

"About a hundred thousand, last I checked," answered Marjorie. "We had a house here ourselves, but we sold it last year."

"Why'd you sell?"

"This island has boomed in the last couple of years, and people from all over the world are wanting to get in on what's going on here. I listed it, and within days a guy from somewhere in Europe made us an offer we couldn't refuse. So we took it." She paused and said, "You look surprised. Why?"

"I honestly didn't think this island had so much going on. I was thinking a few hotels and restaurants, but not all of this."

"Too bad you have to leave in a few hours. This place really comes alive at night."

"Even on a Monday?" I asked.

"This island never sleeps, Alex."

We turned onto a street that appeared to be nothing but high-rise hotels. Ken went about a quarter mile down the street and pulled under the canopy in front of a very nice hotel. The Escalade wasn't stopped fully before a hotel attendant was coming to the driver door followed by a valet. We walked into the hotel lobby as the attendant grabbed the Wellingtons' baggage and the valet parked the Escalade.

"Take the kids to the suite. We'll be there in a little while," Ken instructed their nanny as we headed toward the hotel restaurant. As we sat down, Ken asked, "Are you sure we can't get you anything?"

"I'm positive, Ken. You guys have done enough."

Despite my really not wanting to be there at first, the conversation went very well. I did more listening than talking. The thrill of finally having the opportunity to see these islands I had heard so much about took the edge off my feeling something was a little off with Ken and Marjorie. My problem was, I was a bit put off by how they treated their nanny. It also didn't help that the woman really didn't look like she wanted to be here.

Toward the time it was time for me to get back to the airport, I asked, "So what's your nanny's name?"

"She's pretty, isn't she?" asked Ken, with Marjorie looking on to hear my response.

"Uh…yeah, I suppose she is," I said.

"So are you interested?"

"Interested in what?"

"Ifama. That's her name."

"No, I was just curious about her name."

"Oh…okay. I noticed that you were trying to help her with the bags, and I thought you might have been interested in her," Ken said.

"No, I was just being polite. Besides, she's a little young, don't you think?"

"Not really, but no worries, Alex. She'll be with us the next time you fly us here, so it's okay if you change your mind."

A few awkward moments of silence passed before I said, "Thanks for showing me around, but I've gotta get back to the airport to take care of a few things before I take off to Orlando."

"Sure," said Marjorie. "I'll drive you back to the airport."

Ken shook my hand and said he'd catch up with me next time, and I walked to the Escalade with Marjorie. I had a myriad of questions and emotions coursing through me at the same time. To describe them all would take a week, but the question, "What the hell just happened?"

would perfectly encapsulate every thought and emotion I had in that very moment. My family has always laughed at how my emotions always show on my face. The residual confusion from that awkward conversation in the hotel must have still been lingering on my face because Marjorie immediately started in on me when we climbed into the Escalade.

"You okay, Alex? You seem a little shell-shocked." She laughed.

"Yeah? Nah, I'm good. This is just a lot to take in."

"You sound like the last pilot that used to fly us here."

"Really? Edward and Jack were telling me about the former pilots last week. I think they said they had to leave because their wives found really good jobs out of town or something like that."

"Wives? They weren't married!"

"They weren't? Edward told me they were."

"Trust me, they weren't. Those two took full advantage of what happens on the Tranquil Islands. We're like Las Vegas, baby. What happens here stays here, if you know what I mean?" she said with a wink.

"So what happened to them? Where'd they go, and why'd they leave?"

"Hell if I know. I asked Jack, and he said he got rid of them. Jack and James flew in their place for a few weeks, and now you're here. You're a lot more handsome than those other two, so I think I like your flying better already."

"You think so? I'm flattered."

I smiled and continued to take in the scenery as a way to mask my discomfort from hearing two conflicting stories about why the previous two pilots left. Either Marjorie didn't know what she was talking about or Edward had lied to me. I wanted to believe the former, but I had been bombarded by so many awkward moments with this couple on this first flight to the Tranquil Islands I couldn't escape the feeling that something was just not right about this whole situation. For now, I figured, I will just do my job and stay out of the way because the money I was making was just too hard to pass up.

Marjorie and I pulled into the airport and headed toward the hangars. I thanked her for showing me around and getting me back to the airport in time for my next flight.

As I walked away, she leaned out of her window and said, "Hey, Alex, I sometimes fly solo. Hopefully I get you as a pilot the next time I do," with the tip of her tongue slowly and gently touching her top lip.

"Wow…okay," I said in a tone of disbelief. "But… you're a married woman."

"Okay, and there's sand in the desert. Want to mention anything else not relevant to what we're talking about right now?"

"You come on strong, and believe me, I like what I see—but I don't mix business with pleasure, and what I'm doing here is business."

"Aww…scruples. That's cute. Well, we'll see how long that lasts. You'll learn very quickly, Alex, the more you relax and go with the flow around here, the better things will go for you."

"And what's the flow around here?"

"Whatever you want it to be, baby. I better get back to the hotel. I'll see you later. Get back safe, okay?"

And with that, she drove off. I stood there on the tarmac and watched the Escalade disappear over the hill. The initial "What the hell just happened?" mix of thought and emotion was replaced with a strong curiosity. I began to recall the air of mystery and secrecy that came with any mention of this place. My normal MO is to stay out of the way and do my own thing, but I'd be lying if I said I didn't want to understand the vibe of the Tranquils now that I had access to them. I never had much interest in this place, but now I have a way to get here. I figured I may as well take advantage of it. As enticing as she was, I didn't think I'd be taking Marjorie up on her offer, but I would definitely have to see what she meant when she said I needed to relax and go with the flow here.

CHAPTER 7

About three months passed with things going amazingly smooth. My schedule stayed full, which meant that money was flowing steadily into my bank account, and I was definitely happy about that. Mom and Dad didn't mind me being home, but I needed a little more space than my old bedroom afforded me, so I found a place of my own. Edward slipped and told Marjorie that I was in the market for a house, so before one of our runs to the Tranquils, she gave me a list of about twenty houses and condominiums for sale. I'm glad Ken was on the flights with us because she was still giving me signs that she wanted to provide me with more than just a list of homes to purchase from.

Despite my numerous flights to the Tranquils, I hadn't had the opportunity to stay over and experience how things "flowed" there. The Bahamas was a different story. I had several late flights into the Bahamas and had many opportunities to stay there. Jack and James took care of their pilots very well when they had to stay overnight. We each flew with a corporate credit card to be used only for overnight stays. Rooms in the Bahamas can be reasonably priced, ranging anywhere from $180.00 to $350.00 per night. The same can't be said about the Tranquil Islands. There isn't anything reasonable about the Tranquils. Everything from a bottle of water or a sandwich to a car rental or hotel room is priced in a way that only attracts the higher end of society. More importantly, it's priced to let middle and lower-class people know that this isn't the place for them. A typical middle-class family can save their coins for a few months and have enough money to go to the Bahamas or to Cozumel for five days without hurting the family budget. That's not the case for the Tranquil Islands. What a family would spend in the Bahamas or Cozumel in a week might not get them through a day in the Tranquils. Hotel rooms easily start at $1,000 a night, and things like rental cars and food are priced to match. It doesn't take a genius to figure out that this isn't a place for the everyday Joe. The Tranquil Islands are a playground for the rich, and if you don't have the money, you're not welcome there. Because it is so expensive, Jack and James gave us a $4,000 per night limit if we had to stay overnight. They preferred that we stay overnight if we arrive at 7:00 p.m. or later. Landing and getting the plane into the hangar at 7:00 gave us time to get a car, a room, and take in some of the nightlife, so I was really looking forward to getting an opportunity to stay overnight there. It finally came toward the end of the summer.

On a Wednesday I got a phone call from my cousin Robert about a client from his bank who wanted to go to the Tranquils for the weekend. His client had just closed a deal to convert two abandoned high-rises into condominiums, and he wanted to celebrate. Robert directed his client to the Patrician Gulf Charter website so he could book a flight and then called me to ask if I could show his client around the island once we landed. I told Robert that I hadn't had the opportunity to stay overnight on the Tranquils like I had on the Bahamas, but I would be glad to look after his client while I was there on one condition: Robert had to take me to lunch again. He then slipped and told me that he earned a bonus for closing this deal with his new client, so I told him he had to treat Allen as well because we hadn't all had a chance to hang out since my first day back at the barbecue at Mom and Dad's house. He was so excited about his bonus and his new client he agreed to my terms without hesitating. This worked out perfectly for me because I had promised Allen that we would have lunch this week. I was winning because I got to have lunch with two of my favorite cousins, and I didn't have to pay for it. Both the family man and the cheapskate in me were happy! Just as Robert and I were setting a time for lunch the next day and wrapping up our phone call, another call beeped in. I told Robert I would call him back and clicked over.

"Hello."

"What's up, Archer? Guess what?"

"Michelle?"

"Yes, fool! Guess what?"

"Why do I have to be a fool?"

"I have been trying to figure that out since I met you. Now you're starting to get on my nerves. Guess!"

"What is this…elementary school? What, Michelle?"

"I dropped my papers two weeks ago, and I'm moving to Florida."

"Really? That's great, but why the change? I thought you were going to do twenty-five years instead of getting out in twenty."

"Honestly, I miss my parents. Seeing how well you're doing with your family and your new job made me realize that being close to them was much more important than giving the Air Force another five years."

"Okay, cool! I'm really happy to hear that, Michelle. I was almost starting to miss your smart-ass mouth... almost."

"Yeah, yeah...whatever. You *know* that you know life's not as fun without me! Let that realtor lady who's trying to jump your bones know that I'm in the market and to send me a list. Gotta run, Arch! Sgt. Walls says hello too. Call you later. Bye!"

I couldn't let her hear it, but finding out that Michelle was moving down was great news. We gave each other a hard time, but at the end of the day, I couldn't wait for her to get here. She's like that sister that you didn't necessarily want who somehow grew on you to where you wouldn't have it any other way. Knowing her like I do, she probably meant to ask me if Jack and James could use another pilot, so I made a note to check with them tomorrow when I got to the airport.

The next day began like normal. I woke up at about 8:30 a.m., thanked God for the day, hit the gym for about an hour, and then went for a jog on the beach. Everything was going well until I started having that strange feeling come over me that I used to have as a kid, the same feeling I had when Allen met that stranger by the beach when we were kids. I could never explain it as a kid; the only thing I knew was that I needed to be watchful whenever that feeling came on because something odd or bad was about to happen sometime soon. I didn't let it bother me. I just made it a point to keep my eyes peeled. After my jog, I went home, showered up, and watched the news and sports highlights until it was time to get ready to meet my cousins for lunch. I jumped in the Mustang at 11:30 and headed toward The Dunes Bar and Grill. When I pulled up and walked to the front door of the restaurant, I could see Robert inside, working the room like he normally does and speaking to everyone he comes in contact with.

He called out, "Over here, Alex! I have us a table in the corner by the window."

I headed toward the table and took a seat. Allen walked in about five minutes later looking like a million dollars. I hadn't seen him since I got back, so it was good to see his gut that I'd teased him about was gone. He strolled over with his chest poked out like a banty rooster and saw me grinning at him.

"I know what you're about to say, and you're right. I am looking good, cousin!" he said with a smile. "I knew it must have been bad when I saw the look on your face when you walked into Dave and Jamie's yard. I couldn't let you and Robert be the only Archer men who stayed in shape."

"Good for you, man. So what did you do to lose that spare tire?"

"Simple: stopped eating so much! Especially at night. I cut back on sugar and bread and started exercising again.

Thirty pounds lost in three months, and I'm not going back."

"That's what I'm talkin' about! Now where's Robert? I'm starving, and since lunch is on him, I'm ordering big today."

Allen and I continued catching up. Until about six months ago, he and I were the last two Archer men who hadn't gotten married. I had been too focused on my career to find the future Mrs. Archer, but Allen wasn't. He went through a tough breakup with Anna, his high school sweetheart, about ten years after he graduated. They went their separate ways for several years only to realize that they couldn't be without each other. It was good to hear him go on and on about Anna, but I was hungry and had my head on a swivel looking for Robert. Just as I was about to get up and track him down, I heard his big, booming laugh near the entrance, accompanied by another laugh. I turned to see Robert laughing and talking with some man. Robert is friendly and jovial with everyone, but he is *very* friendly and jovial with family and people who help him make money. Seeing that he was laughing very loudly with this tall White man with jet-black hair that I didn't recognize, I was a hundred percent certain that this man wasn't family, which meant one thing: this guy had obviously been a part of Robert's moneymaking at some point. I expected to see him shake hands with the guy and part ways, but instead, Robert pointed to our table as they both began walking over.

"I thought it was just us," Allen said quietly.

"So did I, but you know Robert. Probably one of his clients that he's working with on some deal."

If I had to describe the guy that Robert dragged into our lunch, I would have to use the word cocky. He wasn't necessarily brash, belittling, or even rude. He just came off like someone who was never wrong, and even if he were, would never admit it. Robert didn't even have a chance to introduce him. Before Allen and I knew it, the guy was at the table, sticking out his hand.

"How ya doing, guys? Matt Arrington's my name. I hear one of you is going to be flying me to the Tranquil Islands this weekend."

"That would be him," said Allen.

"Oh! You're the guy Robert was telling me about," I said. "Congratulations on your condo deal. I hope that goes well for you."

"Oh, it will, but thank you! I hope I'm not intruding. Robert told me you guys wouldn't mind if I crashed your lunch date."

"Not at all," Allen and I said in near perfect unison as we looked at Robert, who looked back at us with a look suggesting he needed us to just go along with what he was doing.

Matt looked like he was in his early thirties and kept himself in shape; the type that either spent a lot of time at the beach or at a tanning salon. He didn't mind talking about himself either. The catching up that Allen and I were doing was cut short, listening to Matt go on and on about himself. In a span of ten minutes, we knew about him growing up on a farm in Kentucky, studying business management after receiving a basketball scholarship to an Ivy League school, and his taste in fast cars and faster women.

After about fifteen solid minutes of Matt's monologue, I asked, "So what hotel are you staying at when you get to the Tranquil Islands?"

I didn't ask because I genuinely wanted to know; I just needed a break from him talking. I was also hoping that one of my cousins would join the conversation instead of sitting there like "The Thinker."

"Not sure yet," Matt replied. "I was going to stay at The Harbors near the beach, but I heard that the action happens on the west side of the island."

"From what I've seen, St. Cesare's has action everywhere."

"Not this kind of action," he said with a rather sly grin on his face.

"Come on, Matt," Robert interjected.

"What, Rob? I'm just saying. You know how it is, man."

After a few of the most awkward and uncomfortable moments of silence passed, Allen asked, "Why don't we look at the menu?"

"Yes…why don't we?" Robert said with a twinge of aggravation.

Now, I would understand Robert being a bit embarrassed by his loudmouthed client's nonstop bloviating. What I didn't understand was why Robert appeared to be more nervous about his client's big mouth than he was embarrassed. If I didn't know any better, I would say Matt was about to let the proverbial cat out of the bag. Even more confusing was the impression I got that Robert was worried about what Matt might let slip out. Robert refused to go to the Tranquil Islands. He wasn't making the money to go every week like Ken and Marjorie Wellington, but he could certainly afford to go for a weekend every few months or so, but he didn't. Robert and Allen are like my brothers. We know each other like the backs of our hands, and I know when something is bothering either of them. After we ordered our food and drinks, I looked over at Allen and could tell he was thinking exactly what I was thinking: Robert knew something he was uncomfortable with, and we needed to find out what that was.

Lunch dragged on for another hour as we listened to Matt enjoy telling us more about his life than we cared to know. I guess his jaw muscles got tired because he finally stopped talking about ten minutes before it was time for us to go our separate ways for the day.

When it came time to pay our bills, Matt said, "Put it all on one tab. This one's on me, guys. You guys let me talk your ears off, so it's the least I can do. Sorry for rambling on. I do that when I'm in a good mood. It was great meeting you, Allen, and I'll see you this weekend, Alex."

With that, he found the waitress, paid all our tabs, and walked out.

The three of us sat there for a moment to dig ourselves out from under the verbal avalanche that Matt had buried us in.

Robert then chuckled and said, "Sorry, guys. You gotta excuse Matt. He's a good guy, but he sometimes comes on a bit strong."

"Yeah, I can see that," said Allen.

"He's all right," I said, "but I'm not thinking about Matt. What's up with you, cuz? Why did you get all weird when he started talking about the Tranquil Islands?"

"Weird? What are you talking about?"

"Fool, quit playing dumb," Allen chimed in. "With as dark as you are, you damn near turned white when he started talking about all the so-called action that goes on in the Tranquils."

"Oh, that? Matt goes overboard sometimes, and I didn't want him get too crazy with his stories."

"Uh-huh…"

"No, seriously. I didn't want him to say anything that would make y'all uncomfortable."

"Whatever, man. We can read you like a book, and something about you was really off when he started talking about the action that goes on out there. You going to those islands and tipping around on Jessica?" I asked.

"I can't believe you just asked me that, Alex! Hell no, I'm not going to those islands so that I can 'tip around' on Jessica! I've never cheated on her and never will. Besides, that place has too much going on for me to ever want to set foot out there."

Immediately after saying that, he looked flushed again, as though he said or alluded to something he shouldn't have. He sat back down in his chair and rubbed his forehead in frustration. He asked for the waitress to come to the table and then ordered himself another beer.

"Look, Rob. I didn't mean to upset you by asking that, but we're your family, and we know when your big head's hiding something. It shows on your face. Now, you may not be hiding something like fooling around, but your big-headed ass is hiding *something*…"

"No one is hiding anything, Alex. Sometimes you just hear things about a person or a place, and you don't like what you hear. That's all. Now if you two are done playing Sherlock Holmes and Watson, I need to get back to the office."

He got up from the table and walked out, forgetting that his beer hadn't even been brought out yet.

"Well, that didn't go like I thought it would," I thought to myself as Allen sat there, still looking at Robert as he walked toward the door.

"Damn! He didn't even wait on his beer, Alex."

"Forget the beer! He's not even working the room on the way out like he usually does. I wasn't trying to upset him. Was I seeing something that wasn't there, Allen? Or did I really see him get antsy when Matt started talking about what goes on over there on those islands?"

"Trust me, you weren't seeing things because I saw it too, but that's not my concern."

"What do you mean?"

"What I mean is that he's not the one flying over there. You are."

"I just want to fly and get my money—so you don't have to worry about me looking for trouble."

"I hear you, Alex, but you know like I know…sometimes trouble comes looking for you."

CHAPTER 8

The next two days would be a mix of sentiments and emotions. On one hand, I was excited to finally get to stay over on the Tranquil Islands. Not having the ability to go as a kid kept me from having any interest in the place. Now that I had access to experience it, I really did want to see what all the fuss was about. On the other hand, the situation with Robert had me bothered. I know what Allen and I saw. Robert was flustered for a reason, and it bothers me that he wouldn't let us know why. We also didn't like the fact that he was upset. He has a very strong and confident exterior, but he's always been a bit of a teddy bear, very easygoing and fun-loving; so if he was upset, it had to be serious. We were going to have to give him a few days to get himself settled down. He took a few days off and didn't answer his phone, so I'd have to see him next week. Robert being upset wasn't the only thing bothering me. He said sometimes you hear things about a person or place that you don't like, so naturally I was wondering what he'd heard. I'd catch up with him as soon as he came out of his funk, but for now, I had to get ready for the next flight.

Friday morning came, and I went about my day as usual. My flight with Matt wasn't until 5:30, so I spent the day having fun. Had breakfast with Mom and Dad. My cousin Nikki was off work, so she joined us so we could catch up. I further solidified my status as the coolest uncle in the planet by coming up to Patrician High School and having lunch with Calvin and Candace. I had to give Calvin a side-eye stare when a few of his friends came up to us and asked, "Is this the uncle who beat those two guys down in front of Kreemy Kone's?" My old track coach, Bill Stevens, was still at Patrician High, going strong, so I couldn't leave the school without saying hello to him. After catching up with coach, I went the to one of the Ford dealerships and got my oil changed before going to the mall. During Matt's soliloquy at lunch, he mentioned St. Cesare having several higher-end night spots where you had to dress to impress. I wanted quality without having to break the bank too badly to get it, so I went and bought a modern fit, solid black Tom Ford suit, with a black shirt and matching black shoes. I went home, showered up, and packed my things for the night. I didn't have anyone to fly anywhere the next morning, so I decided I would fly back tomorrow evening. I'm not a big drinker, but some of the pilots liked to go all out when they stayed overnight in the Tranquils. Subsequently, Jack and James had arrangements with the major hotels to allow their pilots to stay past normal checkout time in case they needed some extra to sober up and fly home safely.

I headed to the airport to go through my preflight checklist and grab something light to eat at Burner's Diner. Just as I picked up my sandwich and began for the door, I heard, "Hey! There he is!" I looked to my left and saw Matt Arrington walking toward me. I said hello as I put a huge grin on my face to appear equally as excited to see him as he was to see me, but I thought, *Wow... I thought I was going to get a few minutes of quiet before his mouth got going.* Thank God he had to park his Benz because I'm sure he would have asked to ride to the hangar with me. Instead, we drove over to the hangar like a mini motorcade, and he parked his car in the pilot's parking spot next to mine. I thought to tell him that he needed to park in the front and wait for me to pull over to the concourse, but given that the schedule to the Tranquils wasn't overly full, I figured he wouldn't take any other pilots' spaces. He hopped out of his black Mercedes Benz S560 and immediately started talking.

I said to him with a grin, "Give me a second, Matt, to go through my preflight checklist. We don't want to plunge into the gulf, right?"

"Oh, right! Sorry."

"It's cool, man. Let me walk you to the seating area."

I returned to the plane and completed my preflight then signaled Matt to come over. He only had a garment bag and another small duffle, so we loaded those up and took off. Matt was like a little kid in the plane, bouncing back and forth, looking out both sides of the plane. There was nothing but a view of a lot of blue water on either side of the plane, so I don't know what exactly he thought would change.

"Alex, I'm really glad I got you as a pilot. You're as good a guy as your cousin says you are. I don't mean to bounce around the plane like a poodle in the backseat of a car, but the truth is that this is my first time in a private plane, and I'm just excited. No one from back home in Kentucky would believe what I'm doing now. Most people in that dump I come from talk about doing something big but never do. They graduate high school, and that ends up being the highlight of their lives. Some go off to school but come home after a year or so. Others go to the military only to come back after a couple of years. They marry someone from school, go to work in the mines or oil fields, start having kids, and that's it. If you talk about wanting more, they laugh at you or talk behind your back. Everyone, my parents included, was shocked when an Ivy League school wanted a small-town Kentucky boy like me to come play ball for them. Everyone but me. My folks didn't want me to go. They said it was too far away. I almost listened to them and turned down that scholarship, but something inside me knew that I would regret it if I did. I knew I'd be just another has-been ball player telling old basketball stories in a coal mine to people who really didn't care. I saved money from my job on the farm for four years. I bought a car, signed those scholarship papers, and got my lanky ass out of Kentucky, and guess what, I ain't going back. So, Alex, forgive me for running my mouth so much, but you gotta understand that things like this don't normally happen for people like me, and I'm just glad that my hard work has paid off."

"So what does your family think about your success now?" I asked.

"At first, they were a little surprised by it, but they're happy about it now. They retired about five years ago and have been wanting to leave Kentucky, so I'm moving them down with me next month. I have plenty of space, and it's just me and my German shepherd, Kody."

"Man, that's great. It has to feel good to look after your folks like that."

"Alex, my man, it really is," he said with a boyish smile.

The more he talked about where he came from and why he was so excited, the more I understood that he wasn't this cocky, somewhat-arrogant guy I had thought he was. The man was honestly just happy to not be in a mine somewhere in Kentucky. I'd probably be just as giddy as he was if I had escaped those odds. The sun was minutes from setting when we approached St. Cesare. The city lights in the distance began to illuminate the dusky sky like the Las Vegas Strip.

"There she is, Matt. St. Cesare of the Tranquil Islands," I said to him.

He eagerly moved to the front of the cabin to get a glimpse of what he had been so excited to see. He rubbed his hands together in excitement before returning to his seat to strap himself in for the landing. We landed smoothly and were motioned toward the main concourse.

As we neared the concourse, Matt said, "We should hang out tonight, Alex. That is if you don't have any plans."

I didn't have any plans other than getting something to eat and exploring the island in a rental car. Seeing that I had a recent change of heart about Matt, I didn't see any harm in hanging out with him for a few hours.

"Sure. Why not?" I responded.

"Great! I heard the nightclubs here are incredible. You don't mind that kind of thing, do you? I love them."

"Nah, I'm cool with it."

"I hope you like EDM because I heard there's this club in the west part of downtown that is supposed to be amazing. Drinks are on me, by the way."

"Sounds like a plan."

I loved house music back in the day, and electronic dance music has a lot of house elements, so I was actually rather curious about this spot Matt was describing. He decided to pal around with me instead of deplaning at the concourse, and he remained on the plane as I took it to the hangar. A baggage attendant gave us a ride to the main concourse where we picked up our cars at the rental car desk. We happened to have rooms booked in the same hotel, so he followed me there, and we checked in, got cleaned up, changed clothes, and hit the downtown strip. The nightclub we were going to didn't open until 10:00 p.m., so we still had a couple hours to kill before we headed that way. Matt was wanting to get his drinking started early, so we decided to barhop on the downtown strip. For whatever reason, I still pictured the nightlife in St. Cesare as having this sort of sleepy, relaxed resort feel to it, so I was kind of surprised by what I saw going on downtown. The streets and sidewalks were teeming with people. Traffic on the streets crept along like rush hour on Monday morning, and the sidewalk traffic didn't move much faster. People were almost shoulder to shoulder on the sidewalk, but no one seemed to care. The mix of slow-moving street and sidewalk traffic provided a perfect opportunity for people in cars to talk with people they saw on the sidewalk and vice versa. It wasn't uncommon to see people walking up to cars and talking to people as they drove along at a slow crawl. A guy or girl in the passenger side of the car might also hop out and approach someone they saw walking along the sidewalk. The two would either exchange information, or one would simply go with the other. At first, it appeared as though many of these people knew each other, but there was no way. Besides, there's a difference in the way two friends or acquaintances greet each other versus people who are meeting for the first time, and it was apparent that many of these interactions I saw were first-time introductions.

My tagging along with Matt was perfect for him. It was unspoken, but we came to a quick understanding that he was the drunken partier, and I was the designated driver for the night. Good thing for me Matt is a happy and gregarious drunk versus an angry one who picks a fight with anyone looking at him the wrong way. It wasn't too long before he had a good buzz going and was going along with the flow. The streets had an intoxicating energy. Being there in the midst of all these seemingly carefree people gave you a buzz without needing to take one drink. People who were normally stiff and reserved during the day became unreserved and loose when the sun set on the streets of St. Cesare. It was as if all fears, inhibitions, and even taboos seemed to dissipate through people's pores as the night went on. Within an hour of Matt and I being on the downtown streets of St. Cesare, they were alive with energy. Music from the bars and nightclubs spilled out to the point that there was music everywhere. With music came dancing, and with dancing came a party in the streets that didn't seem to have an end. You couldn't walk a block without being stopped by a woman wanting to dance with you on the sidewalk.

During one of the many times that we were stopped to dance, Matt leaned over and said with a smile, "This is just the street. I can't imagine what the clubs are like! Let's start heading back that way. It should be open by now."

"Good idea," I responded as we turned toward the club.

"What's the name of this club?" I asked.

"Blue Trance. It should be around the corner."

As we rounded the corner, we could feel the music in the air. The pulsating beat seemed to move through the sidewalk and lead us to the door. Matt was in a giving mood all night, so he paid for us to get in. I expected to be scanned or patted down, but the guy at the door just waved us through, and we walked in. I guess the club owners figured that Tranquil Islands attracted a clientele that wouldn't require or appreciate being patted down. We must have been so caught up in the music as we walked to the club we didn't notice the size of it. This place was massive inside, and it was already beginning to fill up. You entered the club on the second floor which was set up like a big mezzanine. The sound system was so amazing in the place the second-floor mezzanine served as a dance area of its own. About midway through the mezzanine was an ornate staircase that led down to the main level and to the dance floor. People on the mezzanine either danced and socialized or leaned on the railing overlooking the dance floor to watch the action below. The main level was like nothing I had ever seen before. The dance floor sat in front of what looked like a stage with club dancers performing choreographed routines. I had to check my eyes when I looked at it because the floor was rotating. The interior of the dance floor, which was very large, rotated slowly while people danced. People on the exterior part of it would step on and dance, or dance on the stationary part of the floor. The combination of the music, stage setting, rotating dance floor, laser lights, and people created an atmosphere that was nothing short of mesmerizing.

In my amazement, I almost didn't notice an elevator and staircase leading to a third floor.

Just as I thought to go over to check it out, Matt grabbed me and said, "Bro, we have *got* to get downstairs! You see the women down there? We're missing out!"

Before I knew it, I was being dragged downstairs. We got to the main level, and the energy on the dance floor was electrifying. My dance days were long behind me, so I hadn't planned on doing much, but seeing now that Matt had taken me to ground zero of the music and energy of the club, and I began to move with the music. A lot of EDM is high energy, but if you know how to dance a little, you can play it cool, and that's what I did. I wasn't too interested in jumping around like a twenty-year-old, so I hopped on the rotating part of the dance floor and kept it pretty chill. People on the stationary part of the floor danced while watching for a place to hop on when they saw someone they were interested in dancing with. Matt and I weren't preoccupied with keeping up with each other once we reached the dance floor. We had already agreed to meet back on the mezzanine at 1:00 a.m. if we got split up, so we each got completely caught up in the scene. I apparently caught the eyes of a couple of young ladies while on the edge of the rotating floor because they jumped on and began dancing with me. Two absolutely beautiful women. One looked to be Eastern European, and the other West African. Rayna and I were still exploring whether or not we wanted to rekindle anything, so I was still free to have a little fun. These two ladies were a little young for me, so I politely continued to work my way to the center. Once there, I noticed the center was more of the same: a lot of beautiful twenty-somethings. When Matt and I had come into the club, I'd observed the mezzanine had more people that looked my age; so after a few minutes in the center, I decided I would head up there. I made my way to the edge of the rotating floor and hopped off.

Immediately after, I was hit by a sudden sense of familiarity. A smell of sweet perfume. My head quickly swiveled to locate the source of the fragrance before it dissipated. Just as it became very faint, I zeroed in on the source of it: a statuesque Black woman being guided along by a man with his hand firmly on the small of her back. I followed the two of them through a sea of dancing humanity; this grew increasingly difficult as the music continued to energize the crowd. I kept my eye trained on the two of them when they began to go up the staircase to the mezzanine. As the distance between us began to widen, I pushed harder through the crowd to make sure I kept them in my line of sight. They reached the top as I got to the middle of the staircase. As I reached the top, I could see the doors to the elevator up to the third floor begin to open. The man forced the woman into the elevator and moved to the left. She turned around as the doors began to close. Her sad, tired, desperate eyes connected with mine for a brief moment, and my suspicions were confirmed as I called out to her, "Marissa!"

CHAPTER 9

In the moment my eyes locked with Marissa's, so much was said without a single word being uttered. She looked both relieved and desperate, the way I would imagine a person on a sinking boat would look when they saw a rescue vessel coming their way: happy that help is near, but terrified that the help will not reach them in time. I repeatedly pressed the button to make the elevator return so I could go to the third floor and search for her, but it didn't return.

I tried again before hearing, "Looks like you have to have access to get up there." I turned around and saw Matt nursing what appeared to be one of many drinks he had indulged in up to that point. "I've been seeing people go up all night, but when I tried…nothing. I saw you coming upstairs and thought I'd come to make sure that everything was all right." I stood silently for a few moments before taking a seat at a small table near the elevator. Matt joined me and said, "Hey, man, you okay? You look like you've seen a ghost."

"I feel like I have. Just gonna sit here a minute."

"That girl I saw you chasing that guy with, she's gorgeous! Do you know her or something?"

"Sort of."

"Ah…like that? I gotcha."

"Like what?"

"Well, don't ask me how I know, but from the looks of things, she seems like a working girl."

"You mean like a prostitute?"

"Not like a girl standing on the corner that lets you hit it for forty bucks. No, one of those high-priced ones. The kind you find in a place like this."

I thought back to his excitement about finally having the opportunity to come to the Tranquil Islands and replied, "No, I don't know her like that. I'm not into that sort of thing. Is that why you were so excited to come here, Matt?"

"Hell no! I don't need it if I gotta pay for it!"

"So how do you know so much about this?"

"I just know it when I see it. You gotta remember, I went to an Ivy League school with a bunch of nerdy rich kids who couldn't get a girl if their life depended on it. They *had* to pay for it!" He laughed. "I work for what I want. No shortcuts for me, even when it comes to that." He paused for a minute and then asked, "So if you don't know her like that, why were you following them to the elevator?"

I didn't want to go into detail about how I had met Marissa, so I fed him a generic answer about meeting her at the beach a few months back. Matt's a sharp guy, and the look on his face told me that he wasn't buying my story.

"Look, Matt, don't kill your buzz talking to me. Go have some fun. Trust me, I'm good."

"All right. Just text me if you want to leave early. I'll put my phone on vibrate so I can feel it."

At that, he headed to the bar, ordered himself another drink, sent one to my table, and then headed back downstairs. I stationed myself at the table by the elevator, hoping to see Marissa, to no avail. My mind was racing a hundred miles a minute. Part of me wanted to believe I was caught up in some sick joke she was playing on me. Her sudden disappearance that morning before still had me thinking she had pulled the wool over my eyes. Just as I was about to dismiss it and go back downstairs to have a good time, I remembered the conversation that Glen and I had with the front-desk lady at the hotel the day that Marissa disappeared. She said Marissa had come downstairs and turned to the right as though someone had called her name, someone that she knew. Despite how much I didn't want to think about this anymore, I couldn't shake the feeling that something was wrong again. I couldn't ignore the fact that the desperation in her eyes looked even more intense than the first time I met her. Then the proverbial light bulb went on, and I thought maybe the person who called her wasn't someone that she knew but rather someone who knew her. I pulled out my phone and sent Glen a text: "Sorry so late, but I gotta talk to you. Kind of important. Be safe, and I'll call you tomorrow when I get back to Patrician."

Twenty seconds didn't pass before Glen was calling my phone. The music was blaring, so I rushed to a nearby bathroom so I could hear him better.

"What's up, Arch? You okay?"

"Yeah, man, I'm good. I thought you'd be asleep."

"Normally I would be, but I'm working a double tonight. You sure you're okay? Your message looked urgent, so I called right away."

"I'm okay, but I just saw that girl from a few months ago."

"What girl? Hold on, Arch. A call's coming over the radio." I could hear chatter over the radio in the background before Glen was back on the phone. "Shit. Gotta go. Possible robbery in progress. Call me tomorrow." And he hung up. Just as I was leaving the bathroom, I bumped into a guy looking to enter. We both said "excuse me" and walked around one another. He looked familiar, so I glanced back at him as he entered and found him looking back at me in the same manner.

Instead of going back to the table by the elevator, I went to the bar and ordered another drink. I went to pull out my wallet to pay, and the bartender told me Matt had already instructed her to put it on his tab. I placed myself where I could see the bathroom door and get another look at the guy I bumped into there. He left the bathroom a few minutes later but didn't look in my direction. I got a good look at him but couldn't place where I had seen him before. It was nearing 2:00 a.m., and Matt meandered back upstairs as we had agreed. He spotted me at the bar and came over.

"You doing any better?" he asked.

"Yeah, man. I'm doing fine. You wanna stick around a little more, or are you ready to head back?"

"Not yet! This place is amazing!"

"Cool. I'll hang out for another hour or so and then head back to the hotel."

We turned back downstairs, and Matt hit the rotating dance floor. I chose to stand on the stationary part and enjoy the music until a couple of young ladies pulled me onto the rotating floor. Before long, I was having a good time despite the fact that I still had a lot on my mind. After about an hour, I told Matt I would see him when he got back to Patrician. I caught a cab back to my hotel and went straight to bed.

I didn't turn my ringer back up, so the next morning my phone started buzzing around 9:00. I looked at the phone and saw Glen's number.

I expected to hear him answer the phone with some jovial yet smart-ass remark, but instead I heard, "Alex, we gotta talk. Are you back in Patrician yet?"

"Not yet. I was planning on flying back at noon."

"That ain't going to work. You need to get here," Glen said. "Can you fly back now? I'll explain later, but you need to get here as soon as you can."

"Okay. Let me get cleaned up and checked out of my room. I'll land in about an hour."

"Good! Meet me at the Ocean Harbor Hotel when you get to Patrician."

"See you soon."

I quickly showered, checked out of the hotel, sped to the airport, and was in the air in no time. Glen didn't give me much detail, but I was almost certain what he had to tell me was connected to who I saw last night on St. Cesare's Island. I landed the plane, made sure everything was checked in properly, and raced over to the Ocean Harbor Hotel. When I turned onto Coronado St., I could see Glen outside, anxiously looking for me to pull up. He was in plain clothes and pacing back and forth.

Before I could put the Mustang in park, Glen was at the door, saying, "Let's go inside, Arch. You gotta hear this."

"What's up, man?"

"After that robbery call last night, I came home and crashed. I get this call at about 8:45 a.m. and saw the Ocean Harbor on my caller ID. I almost didn't answer so I could go back to sleep until I remembered you called me last night, saying you saw some girl from a few months ago. Remembering that and seeing the hotel on my caller ID made me think you could have been talking about the girl you helped get away from those guys a few months ago. I answered the phone, and this woman identified herself as the front-desk lady, the one I talked to the day that girl disappeared from the hotel. She told me she may know who the girl got into the car with that day. She didn't want to get into it over the phone, so I told her I would meet her here. She's waiting for us inside. I told her to meet us in the restaurant inside the hotel."

We walked into the restaurant, and the front-desk lady was sitting in a booth in the back. She appeared nervous but eager to get something off her chest; a very pretty woman with a thicker build and mahogany skin.

"I'm Officer Hixon that you spoke to this morning. This is my friend, Alex Archer, who was with me that day. You said you might know who the young lady got into the car with the day she disappeared."

"I'm Tasha, and I personally don't know, but I know someone who does."

"Who is that?" Glen and I asked in unison.

"What are you two, twins or something?" she quipped. "Sorry. I turn into a smart-ass when I get nervous."

"Why are you nervous?" Glen asked.

"I'm nervous because the person who saw her get into a car says she got into a car with one of your people. A cop."

"A cop?" Glen asked, clearly surprised.

"That's what I said, honey. A cop. Now you see why I'm nervous?"

A few moments passed, and Glen asked, "Well, how do you know you can trust me?"

"The streets talk, honey, and word on 'em is that you play by the rules. That look in your eyes *right there* is why I can trust you. Those blue eyes say you're surprised as hell right now. I just had to make extra sure before I told the person who saw her that day that he could trust you."

"Well, who is he...or she?" I asked.

"*He* is my brother Shawn. He's a cook for the hotel."

"Where's Shawn?"

"He's in the kitchen. I'll go back and get him."

As Tasha got up to go and get her brother, Glen reclined in his chair. The expression on his face was one of disbelief and disgust.

He looked at me and said, "When I joined the force, I sometimes thought about the possibility of working with a dirty cop. I just hoped I would never see the day..."

"So what are you gonna to do? Don't you guys have some kind of 'code of silence' amongst each other? Covering each other's dirt?"

"I just find it easier to not have any dirt to cover up. I can understand looking the other way if I saw one of my fellow officers break a traffic law or something, but kidnapping? There's no way I can look the other way if that turns out to be the case."

"Okay. I'm just making sure you're willing to run with this because if this is what I think it is, some of your boys are into some serious shit!"

"Yeah… I know."

Tasha returned to the table with her brother Shawn trailing behind.

"This is my brother." He looked at Tasha before sizing us up and proceeding to speak with us. "Bro, it's cool. They're all right."

He looked at Glen and me, stuck out his hand, and said, "My name's Shawn. Shawn Grundy."

Shawn looked as if he had a permanent frown. Shaved head, dark skinned with a goatee, and built like a block of iron—the type of guy that looked like he could dent a brick wall if he punched it. His face seemed to tell a story about life beating him down, but his eyes had a resolve in them that said regardless of how hard life treated him, he was always going to fight for what's his.

"Care if I sit down?" he asked.

We were sitting in one of those large semicircular booths, so we all slid in so Shawn could sit down.

"Your sister told me you saw the young lady that disappeared a few months ago get into a car with a cop. Is this true?"

"Yeah, I did."

"Why didn't you say something earlier?"

"Because this dude is grimy. I got out of the pen three years ago, and he's the type that will put charges on you just because he can. He pulled me over once for having a break light out. Walked over to the car all hostile and tensed up. He was rude, regardless of how compliant I was. Even pulled his damn gun out on me and threatened to say I violated my parole if I didn't calm down. No offense, but I would expect that from a White cop, not a Black one."

"None taken. So he's Black," Glen said.

"Yeah, but I ain't trying to go back to prison, so I stay away from him as much as I can. That's why I kept my mouth shut when I heard people asking questions about that girl."

"Be straight with me, Shawn, and I promise that this stays between the four of us. You doing anything that would violate your parole?"

"Hell no! I have two little girls who didn't have their daddy for three years. No amount of fast money is worth missing anymore time away from my babies. To be honest with you, though, the more time I kept my mouth shut about it, the harder it was for me to look at myself in the mirror. The woman that's missing, that's someone's daughter! I would be worried sick if I didn't know where my babies were. I felt like a hypocrite not saying something about it, so that's why I told Tasha what I knew. I just hope that ol' girl is okay 'cause if she isn't, I feel like that's on my head. I guess I gotta live with it somehow if she's not."

"So if there's nothing that this cop can hang on you, why didn't you say something?"

"You're either a rookie or naive as hell. You hear anything I said, man? This cop is grimy and will put a charge on me just because he can. I have a friend, this cop planted some stuff in the trunk of his car a few years back just because the guy asked why he pulled him over one too many times."

"Not trying to be combative, Shawn. I just had to ask."

"Well, tell us how you saw her get into the car with the cop," I said.

"Okay. I had to come in at 5:00 a.m. to get things set up in the restaurant that morning. There was a banquet that day, so I came in to prep the food for my staff to cook. After about three hours or so of prepping, I stepped out back to get some air. The back alley is kinda nasty, so I usually walk up the side alley to get to Coronado St. When I hit the side alley, I saw this light-blue Crown Victoria pull up in front of the entrance to the alley. I figured it was an unmarked police car, so I slowed my roll up the alley."

"About how far were you away from the Crown Vic?" Glen asked.

"Not too far. Maybe thirty feet or so. Close enough that I could recognize that punk-ass cop. Anyway, so that's when your boy hopped out. He looked like he was waiting on someone. By this time, I had stepped out of sight behind this dumpster because I had a feeling that he was up to no good and didn't want him thinking he had to come at me to keep me quiet about seeing something I wasn't supposed to see. About a minute later, I heard him call a woman's name. A woman walked over, and they had a brief conversation. She kept pointing back toward the hotel, like she was saying she needed to go back, but he insisted that she get in the car with him. She hopped in, and he took off. Next thing I know, I'm hearing all this talk about a woman fitting her description disappearing from our hotel."

"You know the cop's name?"

"Yeah, but I can't remember it right now. I can describe him though. He's kinda short, about five-eight. Light-skinned, like he's mixed with something other than Black. Squinty eyes, wears a goatee or a beard most of the time, and he keeps his head shaved. Not very big but he looks like he works out. Walks around with that little man's syndrome. A real asshole."

Shawn continued describing this cop and other bad situations said cop was rumored to be involved in when Glen and I began to look at one another. It was as if we were in a darkroom, developing a photograph, and the image was starting to become clear. Glen was beginning to put Shawn's description together with one of his colleagues, but I was beginning to put the description together with someone I had seen only twice before. The man that Shawn was describing was the man I bumped into when I was leaving the bathroom at the Blue Trance on St. Cesare's. It all clicked. I had seen him the day before Marissa disappeared. He was one of the officers who arrested Marissa's traffickers.

Glen then said, "That sounds like Beaumont."

"Yeah, that's his name, Officer Beaumont," Shawn replied. "Can't stand his punk ass."

"Sam Beaumont is his name, and honestly, I'm not surprised. He's not too popular on the force either. Cocky and a bit of a prick." Glen turned to me and said, "He was one of the officers that responded to the call I put out when you called me that day those guys were following you and the girl, Arch."

"Which is why I recognized him this weekend on St. Cesare's Island," I said.

"St. Cesare's Island!" they all responded in unison.

"What are you three, triplets or something? Yes, St. Cesare's Island."

Tasha chuckled as Shawn asked, "You rollin' like that, man?"

"No, and neither is Beaumont on a cop's salary. I'm a pilot, so I have a reason to be there. I can't imagine there being a good reason for why he was there. He's gotta be spotting women here to get trafficked to the island."

"Which means that he's doing this for someone. Question is, who is he doing it for?" Glen added.

(I was thinking Beaumont's not savvy enough to head up something like this.)

Shawn then asked, "So what happens now?"

"I don't know exactly, other than keep this conversation between us until I figure out the next move," Glen answered.

"I may not be a cop," I said, "but I know that suspecting something or even knowing something isn't enough.

We have to be able to prove that Sam Beaumont is connected to Marissa being on that island."

Shawn turned to me with tears in his eyes and asked, "So her name is Marissa, and you saw her? That means she's okay, right?"

"I did see her, but saying she's all right is a stretch. I think she's being prostituted out on the island."

"It disgusts me that Beaumont is helping to traffic women to the Tranquil Islands," Glen chimed in.

At that moment, a single tear began to roll down Shawn's right cheek, and he said, "Look, please find her. That's someone's baby. I was too scared to say something, and now she's in trouble. Let me know if there's something else I can do." He then hung his head for a moment before slamming his hand on the table so hard most of the silverware jumped off and landed on the floor. He wiped his eyes and said, "I gotta get back to work," and slowly walked back to the kitchen.

The three of us sat motionless in the booth for a few moments before Tasha began to reset the table.

She then said, "You have to excuse my brother. Being away from his daughters really did something to him. He just can't stand thinking he didn't do all he could to spare some parent the pain of not knowing how their child is doing. He may be built like a brick, but he's nothing but a teddy bear inside."

"You don't need to explain," Glen said. "Your brother has nothing but my respect."

"Thank you, Officer. I have to get back to the front myself. Would you please keep us informed?"

"We will. I promise."

Tasha returned to the front desk while Glen and I sat there, processing everything we just heard. We sat speechless for at least ten minutes before either of us could say a word.

Finally, I managed to say, "We are in the middle of a real shitstorm, Glen. What the hell are we going to do?"

"I don't know exactly, but what I do know is that we have to get that girl off that island. Now, are you totally certain she doesn't want to be there? I know what we've heard, but are you sure we aren't about to embark on a fool's errand all to find out she's been a working girl by her own choice?"

"Desperation has a look, and she looked even more desperate than when I saw her the first time. So unless she made up that elaborate story about being kidnapped in Baltimore, she's in trouble again."

He sat back in the booth, took a deep breath, and said, "Okay, Arch. When's the next time you go to St. Cesare's?"

"Not for another week. I go to the Bahamas on Monday and back to St. Cesare's on Friday."

"You staying overnight?"

"Yes."

"Okay. Beaumont isn't the sharpest tool in the shed, so I know I can get him to slip up and say something. I'll work on him next week while you just keep your ears and eyes open for whatever might be helpful."

"Sounds like a plan. You want some breakfast, Glen? My treat."

"After what I just heard, I don't have much of an appetite. Call you later tonight, Arch."

Later that night, Glen and I headed over to The Dunes Bar and Grill, each hoping the other had some information or at least a semblance of a plan to get things rolling in the right direction. Glen felt stuck between a rock and a hard place because on one hand he felt compelled to help, but on the other, he knew that something like this probably ran deeper in his department than just Sam Beaumont; he didn't know who he could trust. I have a two-beer limit when I go out, so it was about halfway through the second beer when I got a phone call.

"What's up, Archer? It's Michelle. Can't talk long, but I just wanted to tell you that I'll be a Florida resident on Wednesday!" My intention was to congratulate her and tell her how excited I was to have her near me again, but instead, my mouth went on pause while my mind raced. I began seeing a plan come together for my Friday trip to the Tranquil Islands. "Well, don't sound so excited, Alex!" she said with her typical sarcasm.

"Chill out! You know I'm glad your smart ass is moving here. This is great news! We have a lot to talk about."

CHAPTER 10

Sunday rolled around, and I promised my parents that I would go to church with them. For as long as I can remember, it has always been a tradition in our family to have Sunday dinner at my parents' house or one of my cousins' parents' homes. Regardless of who was cooking, the entire family showed up. Devin, Nikki, Allen, Robert, and I, plus all our families, would converge at the hosting house. I hadn't seen Robert in over a week, so this would give Allen and me the perfect opportunity to check in on him and make sure he wasn't still upset. It also gave me an opportunity to fill him in about my weekend with Matt on the Tranquil Islands.

This Sunday was my parents' day to cook, and the church was practically across the street from Mom and Dad's house, so we wouldn't have far to go to eat after service. Church was great, and the choir was amazing as usual. Some of the same men and women who sang there when I was a kid were still singing today. Their bodies were older, but their voices were stronger than ever. Nikki, Allen, and Robert are cousins on my father's side of the family. Their fathers are my father's brothers. They all attended this church growing up, which means my sister, my cousins, and I also grew up attending this church. I always remember my father smiling when he would look over and see all of us in church. Now he couldn't help but smile seeing all of us grown up and sitting in church with him, Mom, his brothers, their wives, and all of their grandkids. Seeing my parents smile makes me smile. Still, with all the joy and love that a typical Sunday morning with my family brings, I couldn't help but feel bogged down by what I knew had become of Marissa. On top of that, I was also beginning to second-guess whether or not I should or even could do anything about it. I was making really good money for doing something that came extremely easy to me. After twenty years of saving and investing money, I was far from broke; but despite what my mother thinks, I do want a family. Making the money I was making from flying these short flights enabled me to save and invest even more for a family. I knew Glen didn't know what to do or who to go to with this situation, but I was beginning to feel overwhelmed by it and wanted to drop it all in his lap.

Just as I was contemplating backing away from the situation entirely, Reverend Johnson began to speak. The same man who baptized me as a child and always knew how to say a few words to keep me, my cousins, and friends on the straight and narrow spoke a message that pricked my very soul. Being the classic African Methodist Episcopal preacher that he is, he spoke about humanity's need for salvation and how to live a life that is pleasing in the sight of God—but that wasn't what pricked me. What he said about knowing to do the right thing and not doing it was what hit me like a sledgehammer to the chest. He finished his sermon by quoting James 4:17 which says, *Therefore to him that knoweth to do good and doeth it not, to him it is sin.* After quoting that scripture, Reverend Johnson asked the congregation to stand up. The guilt I felt for contemplating not doing the right thing where Marissa was concerned kept me planted in the pew. I was disgusted by the fact that I was considering doing nothing to help a young woman I knew had been forced into a life of prostitution. Before he began his benediction, Reverend Johnson said, "The world needs more people who are willing to stand and do the right thing even when the right thing is hard to do. Will you be one to stand?" I leaned forward and looked to my left and could see my niece, Candace, and Robert's daughter, Erika, on the end of the pew looking over at me. Candace smiled at me and mouthed, "It's time to stand up, Uncle Alex." I gave her a smile back, took a deep breath, nodded my head…and I stood up. Reverend Johnson prayed over the congregation and concluded the service. He then headed to the doors of the church to shake hands and chat with the congregation as it left.

"Good to see you, Alex! Sister Archer told me you were back home," he said as we met at the door.

"Yes, sir. Been back for about three months now."

"And you're just now getting to church?" he said with a smirk.

My mouth slightly gaped as I tried to come up with a valid reason for not coming sooner without lying to the Reverend, but the only thing I could manage was, "Uh… yeah, about that, Reverend."

He let me off the hook by chuckling and saying, "I'm just giving you a hard time, son. Your mother already told me you've been flying a lot on the weekends. You got here when you could. That's what matters."

"Thanks, Rev. I can breathe now."

"It's really good seeing you, Alex. I hope that today's sermon helped you."

"It did, Reverend. More than you know."

We laughed and talked for a few more moments before I began moving toward the church steps. He shook my hand, patted me on the shoulder, and continued to speak with the other people leaving the church.

As I made it halfway down the church steps, I noticed Robert, Jessica, and their kids making their way over to my parents' house across the street. Their son, Chris, attends the University of South Florida and was in town for the weekend. Chris and Erika are technically my cousins, but they're around Calvin and Candace so much that they call me "Uncle Alex" as well. I could see Allen also making his way over to Robert.

When Allen and I got over to them, I said, "Hey, Jessica! Can we borrow your big-headed husband for a second? We won't keep him for long, I promise!"

She laughed and said, "Well, I know what that means. Baby, I'll just make you a plate and warm it back up when you three get finished talking about God knows what."

She shook her head, kissed Robert on the cheek, and went inside while Chris and Erika joined Calvin and Candace on the porch.

Robert stared at us for a second before he asked, "Now what do you two fools want?"

"Nothing, man, just checking to see if you were still upset with us."

He looked back and forth at us for a moment and scratched his forehead which, if you know him, means that he's thinking of something sarcastic to say.

He then said, "You two dummies did piss me off being the Black Sherlock and Watson, but you know I can't stay mad at you for long." He lightly punched me in the arm and mushed Allen's head as we left the church parking lot to go to Mom and Dad's house. "So how was your first night at St. Cesare's Island?"

"Well, if I had to put it into one word, it would have to be 'interesting.'"

"Interesting? Not exciting or even fun but interesting?" Robert responded. "What does that even mean, Alex?"

"It means what I said. Interesting. It means I saw a few things that made me raise an eyebrow."

With a sigh, Robert said, "Aw, man…what have you gotten yourself into?"

"I haven't gotten myself into anything, Rob, but my question to you is why would you be worried about me getting myself into something? What's there for me to get into out there, man?"

The three of us stood on the sidewalk in front of my parents' house, waiting for Robert to answer my question. Just as he looked like an answer was forthcoming, my phone rang. I was going to glance at it, intending to see who it was and make a mental note to call them back until I saw Matt

Arrington's name on the caller ID. On the island, Matt had asked if it would be okay for him to call sometime so that he could come hang out with my cousins and me at The Dunes again, but it seemed odd that he would call on a Sunday for that.

I answered the phone, and Matt had a troubled tone to his voice when he said, "Hey, Alex, I gotta talk to you about that girl at the elevator."

"Okay. What's going on? Is she all right?"

"I don't know. After you left Blue Trance on Friday, I saw her come back down the elevator. She looked really shaken up. I had a little liquid courage built up in me, and because I didn't believe your little story about not knowing her that well, I decided to check it out. Alex, I couldn't get your name out of my mouth fast enough before she hugged me and started crying. She pulled me into a corner and told me everything! She begged me to help her, but I didn't know what to do."

"Where on the island is she staying?"

"We were about to get into all that when this huge Neanderthal of a guy with some sort of European accent walked over to where we were. She looked terrified when he told her that she was needed back upstairs. I started to tell him that she was with me when he grinned and stuck his hand out for me to shake it. Now, I'm a Kentucky farm boy with a firm grip, but this guy squeezed my hand harder than I had ever felt. My hand felt like it was locked in a vice. That grip and the look in his eye told me that I better back away. So I did."

"What happened after that?" I asked.

"They walked over to elevator, but before they got on, the Neanderthal called over this short Black guy in a cheap suit."

I paused and thought for a moment before asking, "Was he a lighter-skinned guy with a scruffy beard?"

"Yeah! How'd you know?"

"Long story, but he's a dirty Patrician cop."

"You gotta be shittin' me, Alex! This ain't good, man!"

"I know. Calm down and tell me what happened next."

"Okay, sorry. So after the Neanderthal called him over, Mr. Cheap Suit started eyeballing me. Had it just been him, I wouldn't have worried about it. Might have even started talking a little shit to him, but I kept my mouth shut, knowing that Neanderthal was around somewhere. He followed me around the club after the girl and the Neanderthal went upstairs, so I got spooked and left."

"Where are you now, Matt?"

"At the hotel, getting ready to check out and fly back to Patrician."

"Okay, man. Watch yourself and call me when you land."

"I will. Talk to you later, Alex. Sorry I didn't do more, but that was a little too much for me."

"I get it. Just call me when you land."

Robert and Allen could tell by my expression that something serious was going on, so Allen asked, "You all right?"

"Not really. Those islands have something really foul going on...right, Robert?"

Robert put his hands on his hips, took a deep breath, looked up into the sky, and said, "We need to take a ride."

He went to my parents' door, poked his head in, and told everyone that we were going to the store to pick up a few more drinks for dinner. We hopped into his Navigator and started driving.

"What the hell is going on, y'all?" Allen said.

A few moments passed before Robert said, "Look, all I know is what I hear around the proverbial water cooler sometimes."

"What's that?" I asked.

"Nothing too out of the ordinary. Rich guys going out there to get their thrills with women."

"Yeah, but that's not what you were worried about me getting myself into, is it?"

"No. The crap that comes with that is what I was worried about you getting caught up in. Is that what was so interesting? That what made you raise an eyebrow?"

"You can say that. It looks like women are being trafficked there."

"How can you be so sure?" Allen asked.

I answered by telling them about Marissa, how it looked like she ended up on St. Cesare, and the conversation that I just had with Matt Arrington.

Robert said, "Then it looks more and more like the story about your friend is true."

"What friend?" I asked.

"Your friend Edward Rayless. From what I heard years ago, this trafficking thing started with him."

Stunned by his answer, I then asked, "How so?"

"Again, this is stuff I heard around the office years ago, but from what I heard, he may have had something to do with Rebecca Matthews's disappearance."

"That was his son's fiancée, right?

"Correct. She was a poor girl from the trailer parks in East Patrician. She moved to Patrician after the three of us went off to college. They were together for a long time. Never really saw one without the other. The story goes that Edward didn't like her for him. He thought that she was just some poor chick looking to marry her way into a rich family, and he wasn't having it. Rumor has it that he arranged for her to disappear. I don't know how much he goes now, but I remember him always talking about going to the Tranquils back then. Naturally, rumors started flying in higher society circles that he had her taken there to get her away from his son. Problem was that his son started making his own money in the very same circles, and he went looking for her himself after he heard the rumors. After that, he was never seen again. Now you see why I looked a little weird when you came pulling up in the same car he was always seen driving back then? This man literally signed papers to finance a new shopping development and then dropped off of the face of the earth."

"Any stories about what happened to either of them?" I asked.

"Yeah. Everything from them running off and living in California to them being dead."

"What do you think?"

"What do *I* think? I think my name is Robert Archer and their names are Jeff Rayless and Rebecca Matthews and that what happened to them is none of my business. I also think I have a family to take care of, and getting involved in whatever they had going on could jeopardize me being able to do that."

"Why didn't you say something back then?" Allen asked. "Something could have been done to look into it."

"Say something to who, Allen? The cops? Stuff like this doesn't happen without at least a few cops knowing something, and I didn't want to take the chance of telling the wrong one. Isn't it weird that you haven't heard anything about this man and woman disappearing into thin air? No investigation, missing-person reports, or anything? It's creepy as hell, and I had done a great job putting it out of my head until Alex pulled up in that damned Mustang. I like to imagine them living somewhere modestly with a couple of kids somewhere, but my gut tells me it isn't that simple. My gut also tells me to mind my own damned business when I'm at work, so that's what I do. I advise you to do the same, Alex, but something tells me that your monkey ass is already knee-deep into something, and *that's* what I'm worried about. You do realize that those islands are run by very rich and powerful people, Alex. The kind that can make people disappear. I know you want to help this young lady, but you need to walk away, cuz. I'm serious. Just walk away."

"Alex, I agree with Robert on this one. Sounds like there are more layers to this than you know. Dangerous layers. Walk away from this while you still can," Allen advised.

"I can't do that! What if this were Erika or Candace in this situation? Would you tell me to just walk away then? I don't need you to answer because I know you two would be tearing up the city until you found them. This girl has no one! Her dad is dead, and her mother is missing in action. Someone needs to be willing to help her out."

"But does that someone have to be you?" Robert asked.

"Maybe it doesn't, but if it's not me, then who will it be?"

My cousins sat quietly for the rest of the ride to the store.

After picking up a few sodas from the store, we headed back to my parents' house. The three of us did our best to act like we just made a store run, but it was obvious that something had me a little bothered. No one knows their child better than their mother, so I was relieved to see her being Mom and hosting everyone. With the right look in my eyes, she would have known that I was bugged by something, so I spent the afternoon slipping in and out of the kitchen and making little bits of small talk with her and my aunts to make things appear normal. I put so much attention into trying to keep my mother from noticing I failed to realize my father was watching me the entire time. It was Dad's normal after-church practice to come home, change clothes, grab a plate, and take his food into the den with my uncles, where they'd watch whatever sport was in season. Same with today, and before too long, the television was watching them as he and my uncles nodded off periodically.

In between one of his mini naps, Dad called me over and said, "What's bothering you, son?"

With what was likely the most unconvincing and forced expression of normalcy that I could muster, I replied, "Nothing, Dad. I'm good. Why do you ask?"

With a sleepy grin, he said, "Because from the time you were a kid, you would get chatty and unable to keep still when you were either bothered by something or trying to hide something. I see nothing has changed, so you may as well tell me because I'm just going to keep asking until you do."

I shook my head and grinned before saying, "Okay, Dad. I can't go into too much detail, but let's just say that I have a friend who needs help. I know I need to help, but I'm afraid I may not be able to help in the way that this friend needs."

He looked me in the eye and said, "Son, you can only do what you can do. If you can look yourself in the mirror and say that you have done all you could possibly do to help, then you haven't let that friend down. If you can't say that, then you really have let that friend down. Your mother and I taught you to do the right thing as a kid, and my advice to you today is the still the same. Do the right thing." And with that, he closed his eyes for another mini nap.

I sat and pondered his words for a second before getting up to go outside and call Glen.

When Glen answered, I said, "Hey, man! I have a witness who can attest to Officer Beaumont assisting with prostitution on St. Cesare's Island."

"Perfect! The Tranquil Islands are out of our jurisdiction, so we can't arrest him when he gets back, but we can at least have something on him to start connecting him to Marissa's disappearance."

"Which reminds me…what about law enforcement on St. Cesare's Island? Can't we just tell them about the situation, and they pick her up?"

"Don't make me laugh, Arch! I've never set foot on those islands, but the reputation of the law enforcement there precedes itself. From what I know, calling it 'law enforcement' is a stretch. It's more like a concierge for the wealthy. The most they do is break up drunken fights and look the other way if they see something corrupt happening. It's a rich person's playground, and the law enforcement on that island is only there to make sure that the fun never stops for any reason. Does this witness of yours have a name?"

"Yes. Matt Arrington. He should be landing soon."

"Good! I need to talk to him. I've been poking around at the station to see if there is anyone there that I trust enough to tell about what Beaumont is up to."

"Find anyone?"

"Not yet. Looks like my only option may be to go to internal affairs."

We continued to talk about the situation with Marissa and what options we had when I received an incoming call from Matt. I told Glen to hold on, and I clicked over to see if he had made it back to Patrician.

"What's up, Matt? You back in Patrician yet?"

"Not yet. The pilot had a call come in shortly after takeoff. We had to turn around. Something about forgetting a passenger who had to get back to Patrician immediately. I'm not too happy about it, but what can I do about it, right?"

"How long were you in the air before you turned around?"

"Not long…about ten minutes."

"They should have just called another pilot for that passenger."

"I thought the same thing and asked him why they weren't doing that instead of inconveniencing me."

"What did he say?"

"He gave me some garbage about not having any pilots that could be ready soon enough to get this passenger to Patrician on time and that it would be easier to have our plane turn around."

"Where are you now, Matt?"

"Sitting in the main concourse. They made all this fuss about this passenger needing to get back. I've been in the concourse for twenty minutes, and the bastard isn't even here yet. I just saw another plane take off about ten minutes ago, so that really has me pissed off. They should have put him on that plane and left me alone."

"That would have made more sense unless that plane was going somewhere else. Let me know when you take off. I have a longtime cop friend on the other line who wants to talk to you about what you have seen Mr. Cheap Suit up to on St. Cesare's Island."

"You trust this guy, Alex? You told me that Mr. Cheap Suit was a cop, didn't you?"

"With my life. We grew up together. He's the cop that was with me when I first helped the girl at the elevator."

"Okay. Just making sure. This whole thing has me a little edgy. Probably not ever coming back here. Not exactly the type of excitement that I was looking for."

"Make sure to call me when you take off so we can meet you at the airport. We'll grab something to eat at Burner's, and you can tell my friend what you saw."

"Will do, Alex. See you soon."

I clicked back over to Glen and told him to drive over so we could ride to the airport together. He loved my parents, and he loved my mother's cooking about as much, so it was no time before I could hear him tapping on the front door. He hadn't been to the house in a few weeks, so he was looking forward to hanging out for a while. Robert and Allen were still there. They had joined us in the den when they saw Glen walking in with a plate. Football was on, so Calvin and Chris also made their way into the den, followed shortly by Devin's husband, Mike, and Nikki's husband, Greg. Before we knew it, Dad and my uncles had awakened from at least their fourth mini nap, and the den was charged with cheers, boos, trash talk, and sports debates. We were so caught up in the fun that Sunday afternoon football, friends, and food brings Glen and I didn't realize that two hours had passed with no word from Matt.

"Aw, man! It's 6:00 p.m.! No word from your guy yet, Arch?" Glen asked.

"Not yet. He should have called by now."

Both teams ran a couple of three and outs before my phone rang with Matt on the other end.

"Hey, Alex! We should be landing in about ten minutes."

"Ten minutes? Why didn't you call when you took off?"

"Sorry, man. I was so pissed when I got on the plane that I forgot to call you. I used the flight to calm down."

"Did the other passenger make you take off even later or something?"

"No! That's the thing. There is no passenger! I'm on the plane alone!"

"What? I thought the whole reason you turned around was to pick up some guy who really needed to get back to Patrician."

"Yeah, me too, but apparently the jackass cancelled after making all this fuss about getting to Patrician. Definitely not coming here again. This has been more trouble than fun. We still meeting at Burner's to sit down with your cop friend, right?"

"Yes. He's anxious to talk to you."

"Good! Been thinking about it since talking with you last, and I want to do whatever I can to help."

"Great to hear! We'll start heading to the airport now. We're about twenty minutes or so away, so you'll get there before we will. Get us a table, and we'll meet you inside."

"We're descending now, so I'll go right over to Burner's when we land."

"Okay. See you in a little while."

Glen and I made our rounds at my parents' house before leaving. I followed Glen to his house so he could drop his car off and ride with me to meet Matt. After getting through the beach traffic and finally getting on the road that meanders to Patrician Gulf Airport, an ambulance, fire truck, and squad cars came screaming toward us from behind.

"Must be bad," I remarked to Glen who had a concerned look on his face as I pulled over to let them pass.

Glen said, "The only time we're out this far by the private airport is usually for a car wreck or something. Seeing them rush here at the same time like this is not good."

About a mile down the road, Glen and I pulled up on a crowd of emergency vehicles with flashing lights that were not allowing any traffic to go in either direction. Paramedics were scrambling as the police begin to seal off the road.

"Stay here, Arch!" Glen said as he got out of the car and sprinted toward the scene.

He flashed his badge to the officers that were sealing the area off. A few minutes passed by before I got too antsy to stay in the car. I stepped out of the car and began to inch closer to the scene. I was nearing the scene when I saw a car nose-first in a shallow drainage ditch. The closer I got to the wreckage, the more familiar the car became. A black Mercedes Benz S 560. A chill that would make a polar bear shiver ran up my spine as I came to the full realization of where I knew that car from.

I froze in the middle of the street as Glen came running back to me, asking, "What did you say your friend's name was, Arch?"

"Matt Arrington. Please tell me that's not his car, Glen."

He just stared at me with a look of sadness, the type someone has when they know good and well that they can't help someone but desperately wish they could. Glen tried to no avail to come up with something to say other than what he knew to be true.

He then hung his head in silence for a few moments before finally saying, "Arch, that's his car in the drainage ditch. He's been shot. The paramedics are working on him."

"Is he all right? I asked.

"I don't know, Arch… I don't know."

CHAPTER 11

I'll never shake how helpless I felt watching the paramedics work desperately to save Matt's life as they loaded him into the ambulance and rushed him to Patrician Memorial Hospital.

Glen and I quickly got back to the Mustang and started to head toward the hospital before Glen said, "Wait...why was he here on the road? Didn't I hear you tell him we were going to meet at Burner's Diner to talk?"

"Yeah."

"So why would he leave, knowing that we were on the way to meet him?"

"Sounds to me like something made him leave. Probably the same something that shot him."

"My thoughts exactly," Glen said. "Look, I know you want to be there at the hospital with your friend, but being in the lobby pacing back and forth isn't going to help him. Someone at the airport may have seen what caused him to leave. I think our time will be better spent there than at the hospital right now."

We were only about a mile out from the airport, so we sped over and talked to the security guard at the front gate. Per his normal MO, he stoically stared into the car as we pulled up. I flashed him my credentials and told him that we needed to talk to him, and we pulled into the parking lot near the front gate. Once parked, Glen and I walked back over to the security booth to ask him if he knew what just happened around the bend. In the months that I have been flying for Jack and James, I had never seen this guard outside the guard shack. That said, I could tell that he was a big guy. I don't think that Glen and I were quite ready for what we saw emerge from the guard shack. This guy was every bit of six feet and nine inches, three hundred pounds, without an ounce of fat on him, and he walked like he knew how imposing he could be. My father always taught me to never fear a guy because he was bigger than you. However, seeing a mountain of a man like that walk toward you with a Glock 19 strapped on his hip definitely makes you take notice no matter how fearless you are. He met us halfway between our car and the guard shack.

At least ten awkward seconds passed before I asked, "Did you know about the accident that just happened around the bend?"

"No," he replied with no emotion at all.

"There was an accident no more than twenty minutes ago involving a passenger on one of our planes."

"Happens all the time," he said. "Why are you asking me about it?"

"The driver is someone I know. He was in a black Mercedes Benz S 560. Do you remember seeing that car leave within the last half an hour?

"Yeah, I saw it."

"Was he alone?" Glen asked.

"I couldn't tell. The car that I saw had tinted windows rolled up."

Glen then flashed his badge and asked, "Was he being followed as he left the gate?"

I watched as all the imposing bravado this guard was sporting suddenly dissolve out of his body. He nervously gulped while thinking of how to answer Glen's question.

After a few nervous glances to the left and to the right, he responded, "Not that I remember, Officer."

"You sure?"

"Uh…yeah. Yeah… I'm sure, Officer."

"Okay. You *will* be sure to tell me if you remember something, won't you?" Glen asked while handing the guard one of his business cards.

"I definitely will, Officer," he said as he walked back to the guard shack with far less bravado than when he walked toward us.

While we walked back to the Mustang, Glen said, "He was more nervous than a turkey on Thanksgiving when I asked him questions with my badge in my hand. He's lying, and we're going to find out about what."

Glen and I pulled up to Burner's Diner and parked in front. As I looked through the diner window, I could see my favorite waitress, Julia, inside. She was her normal hardworking self, but she wasn't flashing that smile of hers like she normally did. Since first meeting her in Burner's, she always started in on me with something sarcastic or funny the moment she saw me walk through the door, but this time was different.

"Wow, Julia! Nothing smart to say to me when I walk in?" I asked.

"Hey, flyboy. Sorry for not being my normal self, but I just saw one of my least favorite people, and he just sours my mood whenever I see him."

"Who's that?"

"Well, I don't know his name, but he just gives me the creeps. Slimy little man. Walks around like he's the best thing since sliced bread. You know the type. My waitresses hate when he comes in—especially the younger ones. He's gotta be around your age, but he's always hitting on my early twenty-something servers, and they hate it. Now, I'm older than you, flyboy, so you know I'm not giving you a hard time about being old, but what business does a guy around his early forties have with a girl either in high school or fresh out of high school? Dirty bastard!" She paused to get her composure and then said, "Sorry to get so worked up, but these girls are like a second set of kids to me, and when something bothers them, it bothers me."

"It's okay, Julia. So why don't you just ban him from the restaurant?"

"Can't! The owner won't allow it. We've all complained about him, but the owner just tells us to ignore it."

"Did the guy leave?"

"Yes, thank God! He left after he got into a shouting match with this guy who walked in right before he did."

"What were they arguing about?" I asked.

"Not sure exactly, but I heard the second guy going off on him, something about knowing how dirty he is and making sure that he goes down. As a matter of fact, the second guy was that tall, handsome fella that you met in here on Friday, flyboy."

"Matt!" Glen and I said in unison.

"Ma'am, what happened after the shouting match?" Glen asked.

"Well, they kept arguing for a little bit before the guy asked your friend Matt to calm down and take their conversation outside. I couldn't hear them when they went outside, but I could see them through the window. The guy looked like he motioned for your friend to get in the passenger seat of his car, I assume to finish their conversation. Your guy Matt stood by that slime ball's passenger door. They were still arguing, and it looked more like he went by the passenger door to keep distance between him and the creep, who was standing by the driver's door. It got so intense that Matt smashed the rear passenger window with his fist. When he did, he stepped back from the car door like he'd seen a ghost sitting inside. Whatever or whoever he saw made him run to his car and leave."

"Did the guy follow Matt when he left?" Glen asked.

"Like bear follows honey."

"What does this guy look like, and what was he driving?"

"He's Black but not dark, shaved head, scruffy beard, driving a light-blue Crown Victoria. Can't dress to save his life either. He had to be wearing the cheapest suit I've ever seen!"

"Beaumont. So the security guard was lying," I said.

"What's going on, guys?" Julia asked.

"The guy Matt that you just saw was shot right after he left the airport," Glen said.

Julia's jaw dropped. Her eyes opened wide and welled up with tears as she covered her mouth in horror.

"Is he all right?" she asked.

"I honestly don't know," Glen said. "One thing I do know is that there is something very bad going on with those islands, and I believe this airport is linked to it."

The look on Julia's face after Glen stated his suspicions about the airport and island changed from concern for Matt's wellbeing to one of fear, mixed with confusion about how he could arrive at such a conclusion.

"What exactly do you think is going on at this airport? What does this Beaumont fella have to do with it?" Julia asked.

"Before I get into that, Julia, I need you to tell me more about what you've seen Beaumont do here in the past."

"Typical slimy stuff. Hitting on my waitresses. He talks like he's some kind of big shot. Telling the girls he can fly them out with him for the weekend and show them a really good time. He loves flashing cash too. I told you my girls are like a second set of kids to me, so I don't tell them anything different from what I tell my own daughters, and that's to always avoid a guy that wants to impress you with money and not his heart. A guy like that is always up to no good, y' know?"

"Did any of them ever take him up on his offer?"

"No. Well none of my main girls did, but I think I remember this one part-timer did a few months ago."

"Where is she, ma'am?" Glen asks.

"I couldn't tell you. She was a part-timer and had only been here about a week before this Beaumont fella started in on her. She was a young, pretty African-American girl named Tiffany if I remember correctly. About eighteen. Don't remember much about her except she was from out of state somewhere."

"So what happened with her and Beaumont?"

"She came into work all excited one day because some hotshot wanted to fly her out on a weekend trip. When she finally told us who it was, we told her to not be flattered because he asks all the pretty young girls he sees to go with him for the weekend. I guess he said the right things and flashed enough cash because she left her shift early one Friday after that with a packed duffel bag and jumped in that blue Crown Victoria with him. She didn't show back up to work the following Monday."

"Did you call to check on her?"

"Of course, I did, but she never answered. I just figured that she quit like a lot of girls do and refuse to answer the phone when I call them about showing up for work."

"Did you see Beaumont that week?"

"Yes, unfortunately. I asked him if he knew where Tiffany was, and he told me that he dropped her off at her apartment on Sunday night and hadn't seen her since. I told him to tell her to call me when he saw her again, and the bastard told me he wasn't my secretary! I haven't spoken to him since. He walks into the restaurant, and I just go the other way. So are you two gonna tell me what's going on, or do I still have to keep guessing?"

Glen and I looked at one another for a moment, unsure of whether or not to fill Julia in on what we knew. On one hand, we didn't want anyone to know we were handling this separate from the police department; but on the other, we knew Julia could possibly have more useful information to tell us if she knew what was going on.

Finally, I said to Glen, "Just tell her."

He took a deep breath, showed Julia his badge and said, "My name is Officer Glen Hixon with the Patrician Police Department, and we've recently learned that Beaumont is a part of a sex-trafficking ring in Patrician."

The only way to accurately describe Julia's face when she heard what Glen said is that it was a mix of rage and sadness.

She paced back and forth behind the bar for a second before finally blurting out, "Well, why the hell don't you arrest his sorry ass?"

Stunned, Glen nervously regained his composure and said, "That's the problem, Julia. Beaumont is actually Officer Sam Beaumont, also of the Patrician Police Department."

Julia lowered her voice to just above a whisper and said, "You're shittin' me! That bastard's a cop? Cops are trafficking people now?"

"Not exactly. Beaumont isn't nearly sophisticated enough to run something like that. Matt and another witness have seen him engaging in activities that let me know he's a spotter for traffickers. He's the guy that lures them into a situation where they can be trafficked. They pay him a fee, and he's off to spot the next victim."

"Disgusting bastard! That's why he's always hitting on my girls." She paused to reflect for a moment before tears begin to stream down her face, and she said, "Oh my god! That's probably what happened to Tiffany!"

"Probably so," I responded. "Like Glen said, this guy isn't sophisticated enough to do something like this on his own. He's doing this for someone—someone wealthy. Does he ever come in here with anyone or meet anyone here?"

"I've never seen him with anyone in here. He just comes in here hitting on my girls, but I do sometimes see him driving that blue car of his down by the hangars instead of by the concourses like most passengers do. I always found that odd, but I just figured that he knew someone who owned a plane back there and was just trying to be a big shot."

Glen responded, "He has to know someone back there with a plane. I need you to think, Julia. Have you seen him back there with anyone or leaving with anyone?"

She sat and pondered for a second before saying, "I have on occasion seen him driving out behind Edward Rayless's car, but I don't want to make it seem like I'm saying that he's involved."

"Rayless? The big real estate name around Patrician? Does that mean anything to you, Arch?" Glen asked.

"Unfortunately, it does." I turned to Julia and said, "We told you this stuff, trusting you will keep it quiet. Glen's not telling anyone at the department for two reasons: one is because he doesn't know who he can trust there, two is because we know for a fact that Beaumont has helped get a woman I know trafficked to the Tranquil Islands. We have to get her out, but we don't want anyone to tip off whoever is responsible for taking her there. Say nothing to no one. We're trusting you."

"My husband was Patrician PD," she said. We both sat back in our chairs, certain that she was going to go home and tell him everything. "Relax, you two!" she continued. "He's now my ex-husband, but we're still really good friends. He retired early out of frustration. He would always come home upset because of the upper brass's tendency to look the other way when certain crimes were committed by certain people. Him bringing that frustration home is what drove us apart, but to this very day, I still love and admire him because he was a good enough man to not be involved with the corruption. You guys are doing a good thing. My lips are sealed, flyboy."

I got up, gave Julia a big hug, and Glen and I went to the parking lot.

Before getting into the Mustang, Glen asked, "Should we trust what she said?"

"She hasn't given me a reason not to at this point. She's not who I'm worried about."

"Who are you worried about then?" Glen asked.

"I need to pay a visit to Edward Rayless."

"Well, let's go see him."

"Nah...he's probably not going to talk if he sees you there. I need to do this alone."

CHAPTER 12

After a little back and forth about what to do next, I dropped Glen off at his house so he could get his car to check on Matt at the hospital. By now, he was just as interested in talking to Edward Rayless as I was, but I convinced him that making sure Matt was okay was best. Once I dropped him off, I headed straight to Edward Rayless's housing division. I wasn't exactly sure about how I would begin the conversation, but I knew that this was a conversation that he and I needed to have right then.

I called Edward and told him that it was imperative that I speak to him immediately. I got to the guard shack, and the guard waved me in. When I got to Edward's house, I could see him sitting in his gazebo. He looked very pensive, like something weighed very heavily on his mind. When I saw how deep into his thoughts he was, I considered talking to him at a later time. However, with Marissa trapped on that island, I knew there was too much at stake for me not to soldier forward with what I knew was the right thing to do. My dilemma was knowing that Marissa needed help on one hand, but liking Edward as a person on the other. Despite the suspicions that Glen and I had about Edward, I couldn't help but think that there was a little more to this story than what we could see on the surface. I'm a very good judge of character most of the time, and Edward came off as a good and decent human being. At the same time, I knew that most serial killers seemed to be good and decent human beings as well; while I liked Edward, I knew to be prepared for anything.

"How are you doing, Alex? Care for a glass of wine with me?"

His speech was slurred from the wine, but despite his very preoccupied appearance, he seemed to be in a decent mood. I was hoping to use this to my advantage as I declined the glass of wine and prepared to confront him about my suspicions.

"No, thank you, Edward."

"Good for you. This is my second bottle, and I probably don't need any more anyway. What brings you out here tonight?"

"There's no easy way to do this, Edward, so I'm just going to get right to it. There's a lot of bad stuff going on at St. Cesare's Island, and your name keeps getting brought up whenever I talk about what I saw when I was out there."

While he didn't necessarily sober up when I said that, I could tell that I got his attention.

To the best of his impaired ability, he sat up and gave me his full focus before saying, "I may be drunk right now, but I know this: you need to be careful how you proceed with this conversation at this point."

"Why is that?" I asked.

"Because once you go down this road, there's no coming back. You sure you want to venture forth, son?" he slurred.

I answered quickly in the affirmative despite the chill that ran down my spine when he uttered those words to me.

"So what'd you see out there on the island that's got you so twisted up?" he asked.

"I don't want to talk about the island right now. I want to talk about you, Edward. Particularly, you and your son. Where are Jeff and Rebecca? Why hasn't hide nor hair of them been seen around here in nearly two decades?"

He sat back, looked straight up at the ceiling of the gazebo, took a deep breath before leaning forward and resting his forearms on his thighs.

He then looked me straight in my eyes and said, "You've got a lot of nerve coming out here like this and asking me a question like that." He paused for a second and continued, "You've also got guts, and I respect that. Hell, I admire it, to be honest, son. A lot more guts than I ever had. You know... Jeff might be here right now if I had your nerve."

"What do you mean by that? Where is he?"

"I'll get to that, but before I do, you have to promise to do something for me."

"What's that?"

"You gotta do something that this old coward couldn't do. You've gotta make this right."

"This is your situation, Edward. It's not mine to make right."

"You're right. It *is* my situation, but it's a situation that you're about to know of, and if I know you like I think I do, you'll want to make this right once you hear what I'm about to tell you. But I'm not saying another word until you promise me that you'll make this right." I stood there, caught in a conundrum. To get the answers that I needed, I had to agree to terms that were still not known to me. Edward pointed at his gold Presidential Rolex and said, "Time's ticking, son, and you're killing my buzz. What's it going to be?"

A few seconds passed before I stuck out my hand and said, "Fine, but I hope I haven't just made a deal with the devil."

He shook my hand and said, "No...you haven't made a deal with the devil, but you're damn sure about to confront him. You asked where Jeff and Rebecca were. My guess is that you're asking me that question because you've gone out to the Tranquils and learned about women being brought in for us rich guys. You're a good guy and probably not into that sort of thing, so you did what the last pilots did, and you started asking questions. The answers to those questions probably led you to the conclusion that I had Jeff's fiancée trafficked out to that island or something like that. Am I right so far?"

"Yeah, so far. Is that what happened?" I asked.

"Yes and no. The truth is, I didn't care for Jeff's fiancée. Sweet girl, but not the type of girl for him, I thought."

"Too low-class for him?"

"I guess I just thought he could do better than some girl from the trailer park who didn't know the difference between wool and cashmere. So one day I was having lunch with a group of friends, and we were talking about how good things were going with my real estate projects and some of their business ventures as well when my son and his fiancée came up in the conversation. Jeff had just gotten funding for a couple of beachfront shopping plazas and had a lot of spaces preleased already. One of the guys made a comment about Jeff needing to be careful about marrying such a common girl. We had quite a bit of liquor in us by this time, so we started talking recklessly about all of the possible negative outcomes that could result from Jeff marrying Rebecca. Everything came up, from her bleeding him dry to her convincing him to move to the trailer park. Finally, I jokingly said that it would make my life easier if someone took her in the middle of the night and put her to work on a corner somewhere far away. We laughed about it and kept eating and drinking.

"A couple of days later, Jeff comes to me, saying that his fiancée wasn't answering his calls and that her mother hadn't seen her either. Those two were joined at the hip, it seemed, so one of them not answering the other was rather unusual. One day goes by, and then two, without any word from Rebecca. At this point, even I began to worry about her. I started poking around and learned that a few years prior, the Tranquil Islands had become a landing spot for prostitutes or girls that had been trafficked into prostitution. I also learned that several people that I knew were in on it. It was at this point that I began to get nervous."

"Why were you nervous?" I asked.

"I was nervous because I was a regular at St. Cesare's Island. From time to time, I had indulged my carnal appetites with many of the working girls there. I'm viewed as an upstanding member of the Patrician community. I attend church and sit on many committees and boards in the city. If word got out that I was flying out to the Tranquil Islands to be with prostitutes, some of whom may have been human trafficking victims, I'd be ruined. He and I knew that!"

"He? He who?"

"The devil that you're going to confront."

"Did you ask this devil if he had Rebecca taken?"

"I didn't have to. The bastard told me! Sat next to me at a luncheon a few days later and whispered to me that he had taken care of my 'little problem' with Rebecca. I thought he was joking at first, but I knew him. I knew when he was joking and when he was serious, and he was serious. He said that selling her was the easiest $30,000 he had ever made. I was horrified. I told him he needed to get her back, but he refused. I offered to buy her back from whomever he sold her to, but he told me that once a deal was done, it was done. The only thing I knew was that she was somewhere on St. Cesare's Island. He thought I would be happy knowing what he had done, so when he saw how bothered I was by it, he told me that if I ever told anyone, he would make sure I went down with him. The only thing I could think about was how devastated my son was. He was losing his mind trying to find her. He had become his own man and was making his own money now, so he had the resources to look on his own. By the time I got to his house to try and convince him to let Rebecca go, he was gone. He told my wife that he wasn't going to stop until he found her."

"So did he find her? Are they somewhere in California, living happily ever after?" I asked.

Edward stood up and leaned against one of the posts of his gazebo. He stared at the black expanse that the ocean becomes at night and, without looking back at me, said, "From what I learned, Jeff did find her. She had been assaulted numerous times in the few days she was held captive. She fought them the best she could from what I heard, but to no avail. By the time he got to her, she was so full of heroin that her poor heart just quit beating. Her captors just thought she was asleep. I don't know what he had planned at that point, but from what I know, he snapped." Tears began to stream down his cheeks as he continued, "Pulled out a 9 mm and shot the first son of a bitch that walked through the door after hearing him scream about the love of his life lying dead in his arms. Unless you're Rambo, one gun against many guns doesn't turn out too well. My son wasn't Rambo, so they killed him."

At that moment, I wished I hadn't heard what Edward just told me. He was right. There was no turning back. I was afraid to ask him what became of their bodies, but I had gone this far into this story. I knew I needed to know it all.

"What happened to their bodies, Edward?"

He sat back down, kicked the wine glass, shattering it against the gazebo wall, took a big swig from his bottle of wine, and said, "Those bastards tied cinderblocks to them and threw them into the gulf! You hear me? They threw 'em in the fucking ocean, Alex, and it's my own damned fault! My son and his fiancée are dead because I got drunk and made a stupid joke! I may not have thought she was good enough for my son, but she was a sweet girl and didn't deserve that! Now I have to keep terrible town secrets with the devil himself."

"Who is this devil you keep talking about?" I asked anxiously.

"Oh yeah…the devil," he said in a drunken whisper, still staring at the ocean. "Well, I call him the devil, but you call him James Parker."

CHAPTER 13

I felt flushed. My heart raced a mile a minute. The palms of my hands practically dripped sweat as I processed the bomb of information Edward had just dropped on me. Hearing that your boss is involved in human trafficking is quite a blow, to say the least. I stepped off the gazebo and walked into the neatly manicured grass with a million different thoughts running through my mind. The most prominent was the promise I had just made to Edward. I thought, *What in God's name does this man want me to do?*

After gathering my thoughts and regaining composure, I asked him, "Why now? It's been twenty years or so since this happened. Why are you telling what you know now, and more importantly...why in the hell are you telling *me*?"

"I've spent nearly two decades knowing that my son is dead and that I'm largely responsible for it. What stings even more than that is having to be in business with the man who got this started. I've had to sign deals, pose for pictures, attend ribbon-cuttings, and all the other shit that goes along with doing big business in Patrician. All of this while knowing that this son of a bitch started the process that led to my son being killed. Can you imagine trying to live with that? I've smiled through my tears long enough, and these tears are as much of anger as they are of sorrow. He's gotta pay. But it can't be by my hand, or I go down. You had the balls to ask me about this, so I figure you'll have the balls to move against him."

"So what about Jack? Is he involved in this too?"

"Jack? Hell no. He's as clean as the Board of Health. The complete antithesis of his brother. The yin to his yang or however it goes. James always keeps Jack away from whatever dirt he is into. Been like that since they were kids. Thing about James is that he knows how screwed up he is and has always shielded Jack from whatever he's doing, to protect his little brother from any ramifications that could follow."

"I can't be the first person you have thought about getting involved with this."

"You're definitely not the first person I thought to bring into this, but you're the first person that I've actually talked to about it. I thought about that Officer Beaumont who's always around the airport. I introduced him to James, hoping he was a good cop that would pick up on the dirt that goes on at the airport. Instead, that dirty bastard got caught up in it."

"Yeah, I know. I saw him this past weekend on the island. Pretty sure he just shot my friend who saw him handling a girl who we learned was trafficked out of Patrician to St. Cesare's Island."

"I'm not surprised. James pays him to handle the dirty stuff that he doesn't want his hands involved in. He's why you have a job, actually."

"How so?"

"Officer Beaumont killed those two pilots when they started asking too many questions."

The more Edward talked, the more a glass of wine sounded like a good idea. I honestly didn't think that this could get any wilder; I couldn't have been more wrong.

"The pilots' mistake was that they grew a conscience. I don't think they were going to say anything, but they started getting a little bothered when James mentioned wanting to get back into trafficking children. The pilots knew about the prostitutes because they used to sleep with them too, but the children thing bothered them really badly."

"Children? This guy is one sick bastard!"

"I told you he was the devil, didn't I?" he said with a smirk. "James had this thing about going into different parts of Patrician and luring kids. Now, I don't know exactly what he would do with the kids. I just know that kids would disappear during certain blocks of time. Some would reappear, others never turned up again."

"And you just sat on your ass and did nothing about it? Just let him snatch kids and do God knows what to them?" I asked.

"Look, I may not have been the best husband or father over the years, but I'm not a creep. Any person who would violate or harm a child is the lowest of the low and doesn't deserve to live in my book. I made several anonymous phone calls to Patrician PD, telling them what he was doing, and not a damned thing happened. I guess he has a lot more of them than just Officer Beaumont in his pocket.

What bothered me the most about his thing with children was the type of kid he targeted."

"What do you mean by that?"

"A rich guy in a big, shiny truck with a beautiful woman on his arm attracts attention, particularly the attention of a child. He loved to get drunk and talk about it. He'd pull up in that truck and start talking about money or something innocent like a puppy, and those poor kids would come running. Especially poor kids on the east side of Patrician. He loved to peruse that area. Sometimes he would just go to the east side to observe the kids out there. A better description of it would probably be something like stalking or lying in wait like a lioness on an African plain."

When he said that, it was as if all the blood in my head went to my feet. I felt lightheaded and nauseated because it triggered the memory of Allen walking toward a man with a shiny truck and a beautiful woman on his arm. The hook that guy used to lure Allen when we were kids at the beach was that he had a puppy in his truck that he wanted to show him and ultimately me too when I arrived on the scene. Down to the beautiful woman on his arm, that is the exact MO that Edward was describing as the way that James lured kids. James had to be the same guy who tried to get us to his truck on that day at the beach. God only knows what would have happened if Allen would have gotten into that truck.

I must have looked really bad as I processed this information because Edward asked, "Are you all right, man? You look like you're about to pass out!"

I gathered my thoughts and asked, "What kind of truck did James drive about thirty years ago?"

"Thirty years ago? Why?"

"Edward, just answer the question please. Do you remember what kind of truck he drove about thirty years ago?"

"Sure, I do. I remember when he got it. A shiny black Ford F-150. He adored that truck. Kept it for many years and used it as a work truck once it got old. Why do you ask?"

"Because I'm pretty sure he tried to kidnap my cousin and me back then. You just described a scene from my childhood that I never forgot. A man in a shiny black F-150 tried to lure my cousin and me to his truck to see his dog. Looks like this sick bastard has been doing this for years! My cousin and I were fortunate enough to get away. How many kids weren't so fortunate?"

Edward looked at me very seriously when it turned into a slight grin, and he asked, "Now that you know the type of evil you're dealing with, what are you going to do about it?"

"I have a few ideas bouncing around in my head, but my main priority is helping that young woman that I saw Beaumont with on St. Cesare's Island this past weekend."

"Well, one thing's for sure. If you saw her with Officer Beaumont, James definitely had something to do with her winding up in the Tranquils. Beaumont spots the women for James. If James likes them, he tells Beaumont to bring them to him so he can traffic them to a buyer. It can be for someone as close as the Tranquils or as far away as the

Middle East. Having an airplane service is the perfect vehicle for what he is doing, and he makes a killing doing it. It's like herding cattle for him. If they work out, fine. If not, he makes them go bye-bye."

"Well, that can't happen to this girl. I won't let it."

"You said you had a few ideas bouncing around in your head about how to make this right. What's your plan?"

"It's still coming together, but you'll know when I make a move."

I started to prepare to leave, and as I did, a thought crossed my mind. James being taken down was a lot of risk on my end financially and none on Edward's. I was far from bad off financially, but it certainly wouldn't hurt for me to guarantee that I came out of this with more than I went in with, especially seeing that I was making something right for Edward and not just for Marissa.

So I said to Edward, "I made a promise to you, and I'm going to keep it—but now you've gotta make a promise to me."

"A promise...what kind of promise?"

"I agreed to yours without knowing what it was. You can do the same for me," I said as I stuck out my hand to shake his in agreement.

He looked long and hard at my hand, looked me in the eye with a smirk and said, "Deal," and shook my hand. "Now what in the hell did I just agree to?" he asked with a curious chuckle.

"You've gotta help me with whatever I need to get this young lady I know off of the island and make sure that I can still fly after we bring this piece of trash down."

"I can handle that," Edward said.

"I know you can. Why do you think I made you promise?" I laughed and smacked him on his shoulder. "I've gotta go check on my friend at the hospital. I'll call you tomorrow and let you know where we start."

"Sounds like a plan. I'll be waiting on your call."

The tone of our conversation was serious, but it was nothing compared to the stare he and I locked into as we shook hands before I left to go check on Matt. Not another word was spoken, but the intensity captured in that handshake said that neither man was going to stop until he got what he wanted. Freedom for a desperate young woman was what I was after. For Edward, he wanted one thing and one thing only: cold, unforgiving revenge.

I sped over to the hospital to check on Matt. Upon arriving, I called Glen to let him know I was at the hospital and to get an update on Matt's condition. Glen was waiting in the lobby area near the ICU. The moment I saw Glen, I immediately began to grill him about Matt's status. He didn't have any medical insight, but he was able to tell me about the crime scene. From what Glen was told by the responding officers, it appeared Matt was traveling at high speed when he lost control and ended up in the shallow drainage ditch. Six shots were fired into the car at close range, four of which hit him: one in his left hip, left side, left arm, and a wound from a bullet that glanced off of the left side of his head. As a result, the doctors were still working to stabilize his condition at the time I arrived at the hospital. Glen and I waited and talked in the lobby for another hour and a half or so. Some of that time was spent brainstorming ideas about how to get Marissa off of the island without causing much of a stir, and the other part of the time we spent hoping and praying that Matt came out of this ordeal alive.

Finally, the doctor emerged from the ER to tell us about Matt's condition.

"Officer Hixon, I'm Dr. Mike Sullivan, the trauma surgeon called when your friend was brought in."

"Dr. Sullivan, this is Alex Archer, Matt's friend."

We shook hands, and I asked, "How is he, Doc?"

"I'm going to be straight with you. It's been a rough go. We had to resuscitate him twice on the table. He remains in critical condition, so we're going to monitor him closely. He's young and appears to keep himself fit, so his chances are good. We were able to remove the bullet from his hip, and the one that hit his forearm exited out of the other side. The most damage he sustained was from the bullet that entered his left side. We were able to remove it, but it caused quite a bit of damage to his lungs. One lung collapsed completely, and the other suffered some damage but did not collapse. Things improved dramatically once we were able to stop the internal bleeding into the chest cavity. He's not out of the woods yet. We have him on a ventilator, but as I said earlier, I think his chances are good."

"Thank you, Doc. Officer Hixon and I will track down his family in Kentucky and let them know how he's doing."

After leaving the hospital, Glen and I went to The Dunes to have a beer and decompress from everything we had seen and heard over the past couple of hours. I hadn't known Matt long at all, but his willingness to go at

Beaumont, knowing he was a dirty cop, showed that the guy had heart. I'll take a friend like that any day. I was just praying and hoping that the kid pulled through. Besides his general well-being, Matt held key information that could link Beaumont to a huge human trafficking ring. That may have proved useful sometime in the future, but at that time, we couldn't trust law enforcement here or on the islands. Not having another flight out to St. Cesare's had me a little anxious, but it at least gave Glen and me a little time to craft a plan.

About halfway through our first beer, we realized the two of us wouldn't be able to do this alone.

"So how the hell do we tackle this, Arch? We have an island that caters to and protects human traffickers who have resources that are second to only God himself. This is a tall order, my friend."

"No doubt, it's a tall order, but I think I have an idea. I wish it were as easy as just going in there and dragging her out, but we both know that won't happen. We have to play their game."

"You mean buy her back?"

"If only it were that easy. According to Edward, these guys aren't into that. We've gotta make it seem as if we're interested in having her for the weekend. Kind of like a dating experience."

"Pay for her to come with us. Good idea, but there's only one problem: sex trafficking rings like this usually have someone, or multiple people, watching the girls in whatever setting they're in. They'll be on our asses if we try to leave with her. How do you plan to get around that?"

"I'm no magician, but I understand how they work. Sleight of hand. It's going to have to be all about misdirection to pull this off. We have to somehow locate the goons that watch the girls so we can distract them enough to get Marissa away from them, once we locate her."

"How do we do that?"

"Still working on that, but I need to run. Got a call to make. Beers're on me. I'll pay on my way out."

While I was talking to Glen, I had the general idea about how we were going to get Marissa off the island, but I was creating the details as the conversation went on. The more Glen and I talked, the more I realized that not only did we need more people to pull this off but we needed the right people. We needed a little finesse. Now I just had to figure out how to convince Michelle to help me.

When I arrived home, I called Michelle. Started off with a bit of chitchat to get a pulse on her mood. A good mood meant I could sort of drop hints about needing her help once she got here; if the move to Florida was stressing her out, she would be more inclined to drop her stuff off and drive straight to her parents' house in Ft. Myers. She's as tough a woman as I know, but she's also a daddy's girl. If the stress is too much, she's going to want to go to her folks' house to be babied. The one duty station that Michelle and I didn't have together was when she flew with the Sixteenth Special Operations Squadron out of Cannon AFB in New Mexico. The dichotomy of watching a woman who has the nerve to fly gigantic planes into hostile situations fall apart over a first-world issue like not being able to find a place to pack all her shoes has always been funny to me.

Nevertheless, I knew I had to play this just right. Asking someone, particularly someone like Michelle, to do something like this—she being not one solid day into her retirement—was asking a lot.

Midway through our conversation, she stopped me and asked, "Okay, Arch...so what do you want?"

"What? Who said that I wanted something?"

"You did in so many words. All of these pleasantries and well-wishes, but you haven't clowned me once? I know you too well, Arch. That means you want something. Just like when you wanted me to hook you up with my friend Tanya. I heard so many compliments that day. You even told me that my uniform looked nice! What was so nice about my uniform, Arch? Nothing! It looked just like yours! So cut out all the drama and just spit it out!"

"I didn't need your help to hook me up with Tonya, and besides, she was crazy as hell!"

"Archer, you better tell me now, or I'm just going to say no whenever you decide to stop playing around and ask for real."

I sat quietly on the phone for a second and laughed to myself about how quickly she busted me.

I took a deep breath and said, "All right Michelle, you got me. I do need something, but I can't tell you about it over the phone."

"That serious? You in trouble, Arch?"

"No. At least not yet anyway. I'm hoping you can help me keep it that way."

"Damn, Arch...really? You've been there four months, and you've already managed to get yourself into some shit?

I'm not scheduled to fly out until Wednesday, but you know I can't wait that long to know what mess you've gotten yourself into. Let me get off this phone and call Sgt. Walls to let him know we have to switch our tickets to fly out tomorrow because his favorite pilot has gotten his ass into something."

"Well, since you put it so delicately, Michelle, thank you," I said with a laugh.

"Whatever! Love you, man, and we'll see you tomorrow." And with that, she hung up.

I knew I was going to have to endure one of her rants, but surprisingly enough, it wasn't as bad as I thought it would be. That's not to say that tomorrow I wouldn't get the hurricane of words I was expecting on this conversation. I figured at that time it was best to enjoy the quiet as I prepared for tomorrow. Before I knew it, the TV shows I was watching were watching me sleep on my sofa.

CHAPTER 14

Six thirty rolled around with my phone ringing.

When I answered, I was pleasantly surprised to hear, "Good morning, Mr. Archer. This is Dr. Sullivan with Patrician Memorial Hospital. I just wanted to update you about your friend Matt. We've upgraded him from critical to stable condition. He's still in a coma, but his vital signs are steadily improving. We'll continue to keep you posted."

"That is a great start to my day. Thanks for the call, Doc."

After talking to Dr. Sullivan, I brushed my teeth and started a pot of coffee before calling Glen to let him know about the update I had received. After a couple of rings, Glen clicked over and let me know he had just gotten off of the phone with Dr. Sullivan who had given him the same update.

I was midway through a sentence about feeling confident that Matt would pull through when Glen interrupted me and said, "Sorry for cutting you off, Arch, but I just had a thought. I know we're excited about Matt's condition improving, but we need to make sure Beaumont doesn't try to finish the job. If he knows Matt is fighting for his life, he may try to make another attempt on it."

"So what do we do?"

"*We* do nothing," Glen said. "This could get a little hairy if Beaumont is already snooping around, so *I'm* going to visit Dr. Sullivan at Patrician Memorial and let him know what we suspect is going on. I'll tell him he needs to call me and let me know if anyone out of the ordinary becomes curious about Matt's condition. After that, I'm going to find out who the lead investigator is on this case to see if he's someone I know and, beyond that, see if he's someone I can trust. You keep working on whatever plan you're coming up with, and I'll call you sometime later this morning."

"That's cool. Talk to you soon, Glen."

After hanging up with Glen, I had a cup of coffee and headed out for a morning jog. Michelle had sent a text at about midnight, saying that she and Walls would be landing at 3:00 p.m. and heading straight to their hotel rooms. That gave me ample time to prepare to lay out every detail of this story so they could get a feel for the gravity of the situation. I've been through a lot with those two, and we will do anything for each other; but if after hearing all this, they decided to not get involved, I wouldn't be upset at all. I figured the best way to lay this on them would be in an atmosphere where food, fun, and drinks might help to buffer the impact, so I reserved a spot at The Dunes. It's very similar to Benny's in Spokane, and I think the nostalgia will be helpful. To relax, I went to the gym after my jog and then to the mall to do a little stress-shopping. It had been a while since I flew Candace to New Smyrna Beach for ice cream, but Devin was still giving me a bit of a side-eyed death stare at Mom and Dad's house, so I decided some of my shopping would include a gift for her. I might have overstepped on that one, and it might cost me a couple hundred bucks to fix, but the look on her face when she realized I had taken Candace flying would be priceless. After the mall, I took the Mustang to get detailed and then headed home to take a nap before Michelle and Walls landed.

At about 2:30 p.m., I was awakened by a knock at my door. I checked the peephole and saw Glen waiting outside. I opened the door, and he quickly entered and sat on the couch.

"Something's up at the station, Arch. They're going apeshit down there about Matt being shot."

"What do you mean?"

"I tracked down the lead investigator on this case. Turns out that it's Lieutenant Bradford, the lieutenant that Beaumont reports to. Typically, a detective works on something like this. To have a lieutenant working on it is not normal."

"Do you know him, and can you trust him?" I asked.

"No, and I don't know yet. I've never worked with him, but he has a reputation for being no-nonsense."

"Could that be why officers in the station are going apeshit?"

"It's possible. I know this though: the only time an officer that high up would get involved in a scene like this is to either cover something up or find a dirty cop. I just don't know which one Lieutenant Bradford is up to. I'll keep my ear to the ground on this one until I find out."

"All right, cool. Since you're here, I was going to see if you could come to The Dunes and meet my Air Force friends who are coming into town."

"Absolutely, but I thought that they weren't coming until Wednesday."

"They weren't, but when I told them I had a little situation here, they changed their tickets to come today."

"Wow! That's cool," he said. "I look forward to meeting them, but can they sit at another table? An old jarhead like me can't be seen with too many zoomies at one time. Might tarnish my reputation," he chided.

"Yeah, whatever, man."

Glen and I sat at my place and watched sports highlights until Michelle called to say that she and Walls had landed and were on their way to The Dunes. I gave her the address and told her to we'd be there shortly. We beat them to the restaurant, so we got a table and waited. About fifteen minutes later, I heard the familiar sound of Michelle's voice, which tends to carry over most others. I always teased her that she's the type that has to make a grand entrance, and you usually hear her before you see her. As she and Walls were being directed our way, I noticed that Glen had a stunned and rather-amazed look on his face when he saw Michelle.

"What the hell is wrong with you?" I quietly asked him.

"Nothing. You just didn't tell me that your Air Force friend was gorgeous!"

I shook my head, sighed, and said, "Come on, man. Stop drooling and calm down. We have a plan to come up with."

The exact reaction Glen had to her was precisely what I wanted to have happen when Michelle hit St. Cesare's Island later this week—if she decided to go along. She may annoy the hell out of me at times, but she has always been a head-turner. She has that model look that a lot of guys go crazy for. Her father is Black, and her mother is half White and half Mexican; stands about five feet and nine inches, with spirally black hair, and keeps herself in shape. It bothers her sometimes, but men gawk wherever she goes. Even more than the situation that I was about to explain to her, my asking her to play up how she looks might really piss her off.

"Wow, Arch! Three months out of my sight, and you're already having problems. What have you gotten yourself into?" she asked.

"Nice to see you too, Michelle, and yeah... I'm okay too. Thanks for asking!" I responded while she hugged me. "Walls, how are you doing, man? So glad to see you."

"I'm good, Major!" he said with his trademark smile. "You know I wasn't gonna hear about you having trouble and not be here to help."

"I appreciate you coming, man. I really do." I pointed at Glen and said, "Michelle, Patrick...this is my good friend, Glen Hixon, with the Patrician Police Department. We've known each other since we were kids."

I gave Glen a slight nudge to help Glen break his infatuated gaze enough to finally acknowledge and properly greet them. We all sat down and ordered a late lunch as I began to explain Marissa's situation and how Matt was recovering in the hospital as a result of it. I went on to divulge to Michelle and Patrick how I needed their help to get Marissa off of the island and the roles that I wanted them to play in making that happen. Glen chimed in and detailed the Beaumont issue and the problem with going to Patrician PD.

The two sat quietly for several minutes, stunned and somewhat perplexed by what they had just heard. Michelle typically wears her emotions on her face, so it's usually not hard to tell what's on her mind. That being said, the look she had while processing this information was one I had never seen on her in all the years I had known her. Patrick looked shocked, but Michelle looked angry, hurt, and saddened on one hand but scared, worried, and confused on the other.

She wiped a tear from the corner of her eye and said, "I didn't know what to expect when you said you needed our help, but never in a million years would I have imagined something like this."

"Major, I've heard of things like this happening, but I didn't think it was real. This is a lot to take in," Walls added.

A few more moments passed where no one said a word.

Just as I was about to tell them that I understood if they didn't have it in them to help out, Michelle wiped another tear from her eye and asked, "So when do we start?"

I breathed a sigh of relief because I was not so sure how well I'd be able to pull this off going in solo.

I asked, "That easy? You sure?"

"I can't say no to this, Arch. This is someone's life we're talking about. I wouldn't be able to sleep at night or look at myself in the mirror if I knowingly turned my back on this situation and didn't at least try to help. I'm in."

"Walls...you in?" I asked.

"Major, you've done so much for me both personally and in my career. There's no way I'd say no. I'd follow you anywhere, sir, but how do you plan on extracting her?"

"That's the problem. I've never done an extraction."

"I have, sir."

"Really?"

"Who do you think I was dropping off sometimes back when I was flying with the 16th Spec. Ops Squadron?" Michelle said with a smile while pointing at Walls with her thumb.

"So how do we pull this off, Walls?" I asked.

"Well, the first thing we have to do is some surveillance of the scene. Gotta get a feel for the layout of the area where we'll be operating. You said you saw her in a club called The Blue Trance on a Friday night, correct?"

"Right."

"Do you think this is the only place they have her operating out of?"

"I wouldn't know."

"That's the first thing we have to find out. Do you have a picture of her?"

"Unfortunately, I don't. She never made it to the police station."

"I could probably get a surveillance video from the hotel where she stayed," Glen offered.

"Okay, I'll need that ASAP."

"I'm on it," Glen said. "Meantime, I need to head back to the hospital to check on Matt and to see if Beaumont has caught wind that Matt isn't dead yet."

We discussed a few more details and potential scenarios both in Patrician and on the Tranquil Islands when Michelle said, "You know, this Beaumont guy could be a problem. He sounds like a loose cannon, but from the way you described him at this Blue Trance place, he's all about business when he's there. This Neanderthal guy probably keeps him in check. He may need to be distracted before he gets there."

"How do you propose that?"

"A girl has her ways," she said with a wink. "Just get me in front of this loser, and I'll do the rest."

"I'm sure I can help with that," Glen said with a grin.

Michelle and Glen began to talk among themselves about Beaumont and how he operated in Patrician and on the island. While they talked, Patrick and I began to talk more about what it would take to get Marissa off of the island safely. We agreed that the best way to do it would obviously be quietly and without incident. The dilemma we kept running into in the discussion was not having ample time to really surveil and prepare. Arriving fresh on a Friday night and trying to extract someone from a monitored location could be disastrous.

"Do you have anyone else here that can go to the island and surveil earlier than Friday, Major?" Patrick asked.

"I don't."

"No worries, Major. I have an uncle who I'm sure will be down to help."

"He's experienced in this type of thing?"

"You have no idea, Major. If it could be done in the Air Force, my uncle Charles has done it. He'll love this."

"What's he do now?"

"He's been running a rental car agency in Spokane since he retired from the Air Force."

"Really? I met a Charles who ran the rental car agency where I got the car I drove here when I retired, but he was sixty-something. White guy."

"Then it sounds like you met him."

"So how does a guy as dark as you and me get a White uncle? He marry into the family?"

"Yeah. Married my aunt Anita when he first went into the Air Force, back when interracial marriages weren't as accepted as they are now. He was one of my favorite people when I was growing up. When Aunt Anita passed away, I remember Uncle Chuck coming up to me after the funeral and telling me that my aunt no longer being with us changed nothing. For me and my brothers and cousins, he would always be Uncle Chuck. My family loves him to pieces, so they wrapped their arms around him when my aunt passed. He's at all the family reunions and over on the holidays."

"Okay. Well, we have to get him onto the island."

"Definitely—but from what I know, the Tranquil Islands are for superrich people, Major. Uncle Chuck ain't broke, but he's not rolling in money like that."

"He doesn't need to worry about that. I have that covered. Just find out how soon he can be here."

After Patrick and I finished talking, I focused my attention back on Glen and Michelle's conversation. Despite all the hearts popping over his head like a cartoon character when he's shot by Cupid's arrow, Glen managed to come up with a fairly decent plan to get Michelle in front of Beaumont before Friday. Glen often described Beaumont as not being the sharpest tool in the shed; he was an egotistical asshole who somehow believed himself to be God's gift to the female gender. His plan was to get an idea for Beaumont's routine and schedule for this week and have him and Michelle "casually" bump into each other somewhere.

I've seen Michelle in scenarios like this before. Guys would fawn over her at Benny's while trying to take her home. She'd have zero interest in them, but they would persist. Her thoughts then were that if they wouldn't take the hint and kept trying to take her home, she would at least get drinks and food out of it to compensate for the aggravation she had to endure. I've seen her charm the socks off anyone from bank presidents to politicians. By the time she was done with them, they were offering to take her all over the world. She even got me a couple of meals and drinks courtesy of some of her hapless admirers just to show me she could. I knew Beaumont would be in trouble if he was as dense as Glen described him. Gathering info about Beaumont's routines would also give Glen the opportunity to get a feel for whether or not Lieutenant Bradford was dirty. Bradford being a good cop could be advantageous in getting Beaumont convicted. If Bradford turned out to be dirty, the scenario would inevitably become complicated. For now, we just agreed that Glen's focus was to get Michelle in front of Beaumont to see whether or not he would be on St. Cesare's Island this weekend.

After lunch, Glen made his way to the hospital to talk with Dr. Sullivan about Matt's condition. Meanwhile, Walls went to his hotel room to talk to Chuck, and Michelle and I went to my parents' house. Michelle, Devin, Nikki, and Jessica hit it off twenty years ago when they met, so they were excited to reconnect when they heard Michelle would be here this week. Six thirty rolled around, and I got a call from Walls saying that Chuck was game for whatever we had planned. I then contacted Edward to let him know that I needed to see him. He told me to come over.

When I arrived at his house, he met me at the fountain in front and invited me inside.

"Good to see you Alex!" he said. "I take it this means your plan is coming along nicely, and you need something to help it along."

"That's exactly what it means," I answered as Edward slid me a beer across his kitchen island. "I have a surveillance guy that I need to get here and then over to St. Cesare's Island ASAP. How soon could you make that happen?"

"Where is he?"

"Spokane, Washington."

"You want him here tonight or in the morning?" he queried.

I looked at Edward with a blank stare for a second, stunned at how easily he said that; I guess I forgot for a moment that I was talking to a multimillionaire.

"Tonight then."

"Okay. Tell your guy to pack his shit, and I can have him in the air as soon as he's ready."

I immediately called Walls and told him to give me Chuck's number so that I could connect him with Edward.

Walls responded, "I can already tell you, Major, that won't work with Uncle Chuck. He doesn't give his number out to people he works with like this. He's a 'don't contact me, I'll contact you' kind of guy with this kind of thing. Real *Spy Games* type shit. More than any I've ever been involved with. He already told me to tell you and whoever else I'm working with that we need to watch for incoming calls from unusual phone numbers because they will likely be him calling if he needs something."

I gave Edward's number to Walls, and within a minute, Edward's phone rang. Chuck gave him specific information on how and where to book his tickets, rent his cars, and reserve his hotel rooms for both Patrician and St. Cesare's Island. Chuck was in the air within the hour.

CHAPTER 15

A light rain had begun to fall shortly before Glen arrived at Patrician Memorial Hospital. On his way there, Glen called Dr. Sullivan to confirm that he would be at the hospital when Glen arrived.

No sooner than he'd parked his car, a text message from Dr. Sullivan dinged Glen's phone, asking, "Are you close?"

Glen's response was, "Yes. I'm in the parking lot. Is everything okay?"

"I'm hoping you can tell me."

Upon reading Dr. Sullivan's response, Glen quickly trotted into the hospital and made his way to Dr. Sullivan's office.

"Is everything okay, Doc?" Glen asked.

"You told me to contact you if anyone came to the hospital, asking about your friend Matt. Someone came in stating that he was a police officer and started asking questions."

"Were they investigative questions?"

"Yes and no. The questions were more geared toward knowing if Matt would live or die, would he be able to talk. That's normal. What wasn't normal was how this cop appeared to be somewhat disappointed when I told him that Matt's condition was steadily improving. No matter how hard he tried to appear objective, he was clearly bothered when I told him that Matt was improving."

"Can you describe this cop, Doc?"

"Sure. African American, about five-nine, fit, scruffy beard, shaved head."

"Did he leave you his card?"

"No, which I thought was odd. He just left when I gave him the update on Matt's condition. I texted you the moment he left my office because it just felt off."

"So he literally just left?"

"Yes. I'm surprised you didn't run into him on your way in."

"He may still be here. I'll be right back, Doc."

Glen began to walk around the lobby area to see if he saw Beaumont walking around or talking to anyone. Then the idea to check the bathroom hit him, and he began to walk toward the men's room. Glen got about halfway down the hall from it when Beaumont emerged from the bathroom. Both stopped dead in their tracks and stared at one another for a brief moment. Glen casually acknowledged Beaumont, who in turn acknowledged Glen with a somewhat-guilty demeanor.

Observing this, Glen approached him and asked, "Officer Beaumont. What brings you out this way?"

"Oh…nothing. Just looking into the condition of a victim of an attempted murder."

"Wouldn't be the guy who got shot by Patrician Gulf Airport, would it?"

"Yeah. Unfortunate what happened to him."

"Definitely was, but I thought Lieutenant Bradford was handling the investigation."

Stunned by Glen's response, Beaumont began to get nervous. He got fidgety and sweat began to bead on his forehead.

Desperate to escape the awkwardness, Beaumont blurted out, "Yeah, he is. I just thought I would check in on the victim and let Bradford know what I found out." He paused briefly and asked, "Wait. What are you doing here?"

Without batting an eye and as convincing as a top defense attorney, Glen answered, "A friend of mine had an allergic reaction to shellfish, and I had to bring her to the hospital." Certain that he knew Beaumont was lying about gathering information for Lieutenant Bradford, Glen said, "Good seeing you, Officer Beaumont. I'm just going to sit and wait for my friend Lisa to get released. Have a good night."

He then took a seat in the waiting room to be able to see what Beaumont would do next. As expected, Beaumont nervously left the hospital waiting room, jumped in his car, and left.

Late the next morning, the five of us met at The Dunes to share any current information we had and to come up with a more-concrete plan of action to get Marissa off of St. Cesare's Island.

They all, except Chuck, had a weariness about them. At the same time, there was an air of relentlessness and even optimism at our table. Though we weren't exactly sure how, we were positive that the sun was going to eventually shine on this situation. The first thing we were certain must be done was to get Chuck onto the island so that he could begin to spy out the land. Next, we had to somehow locate Beaumont that day and put Michelle on him to get him to loosen up and possibly give us some information about what went on behind closed doors at The Blue Trance.

At this point in the plan, Chuck turned to Glen and asked, "Is there a way for you to do this without looking suspicious?"

"Probably not. He was a nervous wreck last night when I questioned him about being at the hospital. It's not like I know the guy that well, so it may look a little odd if I start asking about him around the station."

"Not a problem," Chuck said. "Give me a second."

He stepped away from the table and jumped on his phone. While Chuck talked, the remaining four of us thought it best to have Walls tail Michelle while she was working Beaumont in the event she needed help. That left Glen and me with not a lot to do other than wait until Friday. That obviously didn't sit right with either of us, so we continued to brainstorm about what more could be done.

After about ten minutes, Chuck walked back to the table and said that Beaumont would be working the west side near the boardwalk on Coronado Street this evening. He went on to tell us that he would likely be in plain clothes, popping in and out of a bar in the area named Pelican's during his shift. Michelle, Glen, and I paused and perplexedly looked at one another, baffled by how quickly Chuck gathered the intel he just gave us. Information is power, but information backed by speed is power without measure.

Convinced that there must be some covert method he used to gather that information so rapidly, Glen asked, "I work in the same station with the guy, and I didn't know that. Do you have someone on the inside feeding you information?"

"No. I just asked the secretary," Chuck said with a laugh.

"You've gotta be shittin' me," Glen said.

"Yeah…a little bit. I told her a little fib. Edward told me a little bit about this guy when I landed, so I looked him up at the hotel. I told her I was an old Army buddy of Beaumont's, was passing through Patrician, and I wanted to surprise him—and she sang like a canary. You should probably get a new secretary though. That was too easy." Chuck reached down and grabbed his beer, drank the last little bit in the bottle, and asked Glen, "Do you have the picture of Marissa?"

When Glen handed him the picture, Chuck said, "Well, I better get going. I take off to St. Cesare's in about two hours. I'll be in touch as soon as I know something."

As evening neared, Michelle and Walls headed over toward Pelican's Bar near the boardwalk on Coronado St. After talking to Glen, they knew to be on the lookout for Beaumont's Crown Victoria, so they staked out on Coronado St. near the bar. At about 6:15, I received a text from Michelle: a snapshot of a man walking into Pelican's with a message asking, "Is this him?" I confirmed the man in the picture was Beaumont. Her response was, "Okay. I got him. Hit you back later, Arch." Michelle waited about ten minutes before following Beaumont into the bar to give him a second to get comfortable.

When she entered, I got the exact reaction I was hoping for: the very air was sucked out of the room as she walked in. Every man turned and stared as she walked to the right side of the bar opposite of where Beaumont was sitting. By placing herself there, she could have a view of Beaumont as well as a clear view of the door and the entire establishment. She ordered a Crown Royal and Coke and watched the evening running of *SportsCenter* as she waited for her drink. While waiting, she surveyed the scene as if taking in the ambiance and briefly caught eyes with Beaumont, who already had a bead on her like a leopard on a savannah wildebeest. Michelle gave him a look to suggest she was interested and wanted conversation but was too much of a lady to make the first move. He didn't move on the first glance, but after her second and more-focused look at him while sipping her Crown and Coke, he walked over like a lamb that was unknowingly being led to the slaughterhouse. His fake tough-guy stroll did little to hide his corny demeanor, making it difficult for Michelle to not crack up laughing as he rounded the bar and took a seat next to hers. He wasted no time and got right into hitting on her.

"I couldn't help but notice how beautiful you were when you walked through the door," he said.

"Oh, please. You probably say that to all the girls. Besides, a good-looking guy like you must have a woman anyway."

"Me? No. I'm single."

"Really?" she said with a hint of eagerness. She eased back and said, "I just find that hard to believe."

"Why's that?"

"You just seem like a guy who sees what he wants and goes after it. It's been my luck that the bold, handsome ones like you always have a woman. When I saw you over there, I told myself not to get my hopes up because you're likely taken anyway."

"No need to worry about that. I'm definitely single." She could tell by the look in his eye and by how quickly he acknowledged that he was single that he was hers to play with. "So are you new in town? I've never seen you in here before," he continued.

"Sort of. I'm in town from Chicago, scouting out some potential homes. I recently retired from Boeing's corporate office and am looking at possibly relocating to Patrician."

"Retired? You don't look old enough to retire."

"Well, technically I am kind of young for retirement, but my story is a little different. I went to work for Boeing right after high school and did office work for them. They had a program that paid for an employee's education if they would commit to five years of employment after graduation, so I couldn't pass that up. I thought at first I would work the five years and then move on to something else, but they treated me really well, and the money was great, so I stayed a little longer. Five years turned to ten, then to twenty, and now I'm here talking to you, handsome."

With the tone of a schoolboy with a crush on his teacher, Beaumont asked, "What did you do for them after you graduated college?"

"I did marketing and sales, but now I'm bored with it. They offered early retirement for people like me. I figured my Boeing pension plus my investments would be more than enough for me, so I took it. Now I'm here talking to a sexy Florida man before I go visit the Tranquil Islands to let loose a bit."

"The Tranquil Islands? You must have done very well for yourself if you're letting loose out there," he said.

"You familiar with those islands? I hadn't heard much about them until a few weeks ago."

"You could say that. I am one of the heads of security on the weekends at a night spot there called The Blue Trance."

"You're a good person to know then. I read about that place when I was deciding on where to go for vacation. Makes sense that a strong, handsome guy like you would be the head of security there. Will you be there this weekend?"

"I definitely will."

"Well, make some time for a new friend this weekend if you can," she said with a wink as she sipped her Crown and Coke again.

Walls walked in unnoticed and took a seat at a table by the entrance. He later said that by the time he walked in, Michelle looked like a cat, and Beaumont looked like a new toy she had been given to play with, batting him back and forth with her words. After a few more drinks and strokes to his massive ego, Beaumont told Michelle about the rooms in The Blue Trance in which he could show her a good time. More importantly, he let slip what goes on in the upper part of the club, that it was where a lot of high-stakes gambling, among other things, took place. Many of the high rollers there had women brought up for "entertainment," as he put it. He went on to tell her that the upper part was an "anything goes" environment and that he would love to show her how things work up there.

Knowing that she had him hooked like a bass on a line, she said, "Hmmm. Anything goes, you say? Let me think about it."

"When will I know something?" he asked.

"Patience, cowboy. I promise I won't make you wait too long. What's your phone number?" He desperately signaled to the bartender to bring him a pen. He grabbed a napkin and scribbled down his number. Michelle smiled and said, "You could have just told it to me, and I would have put it in my phone."

"Oh, yeah. Sorry. I guess you have me a little nervous."

"It's okay. It's kind of cute." She put her phone back in her purse, finished her drink, and said, "Talk to you soon, handsome," as she kissed him on his cheek and walked toward the front door.

She noticed Walls at his table, shaking his head with his lips balled up, desperately trying not to laugh at how badly she had Beaumont twisted up.

Later that evening, Michelle told Chuck to send Beaumont a text message from one of his random numbers, saying she had decided to let him show her the upper part of The Blue Trance when she arrived on St. Cesare's Island. This prompted Chuck to focus his attention on that part of The Blue Trance a little closer during his surveillance.

CHAPTER 16

Early Thursday morning, I received a call from Chuck, asking me to gather everyone in one location so he could brief us on what he had learned so far. We met at Edward's house to listen to Chuck's intel.

He explained, "The upper part of The Blue Trance is far more extensive than it appears from the street. The third floor is a large, open, high-stakes gambling hall that looks like any casino one would see in Las Vegas. There are women stationed throughout the second floor of the club who strike up conversations with men who look like they're there for more than just music and drinks, and they invite them upstairs. The only way to get up to the third floor is to either pay the bartender or be escorted up by one of the club women. Once upstairs, the woman who got the guy there either stays with him or casually pawns him off to another girl who specifically works in the upper part of the club.

"Here is where it got tricky: I got curious when I noticed a back entrance to the upper part where women were consistently going in and out with men. After a few games of blackjack, I wandered back there as though I was looking for the restroom. What I saw back there was a skyway connecting The Blue Trance to another building. I started to venture over but thought better of it and turned around. I started to head back toward The Blue Trance until I saw the door open across the skyway.

"A very large man stuck his head out the door and said, 'You're heading the right direction. Just come over.' I told him I was looking for the bathroom which made him look confused. He stepped out of the door and began to walk across the skyway toward me. Halfway across, he asked, 'You don't want a girl?' with an Eastern European accent.

"'Well, of course, I want a girl. I just need to pee first.'

"The guy stood silently for a second, as if he were trying to figure something out about me. He stepped closer to me, which honestly made me a little nervous on account of his being a gigantic son of a bitch.

"He pointed behind himself and said, 'Bathroom in here too. You don't see girls you like in front?'

"I breathed a sigh of relief inside because I thought that he was on to me and said, 'Not really.'

"'Well, what do you like? We have all kinds.' I gave him as close a description to Marissa as I could, to which he responded, 'I have a perfect girl for you. She doesn't talk a lot, but she will make you really happy.' He pointed me across the skyway and said, 'Go use the bathroom inside. I will be right back with a girl for you.'

"I crossed the skyway and entered the building on the other side. It was a hotel that appears to be used strictly for prostitution. An attendant is positioned at the entrance to take your money. Edward made sure I had plenty of money, so I paid what he asked. He gave me the key to a room, so

I went there and waited for that big bastard to come back. I knew it was a long shot, but I was hoping he would come back with Marissa so I wouldn't have to do more searching for her. I counted on the room being bugged or wired with some sort of hidden video surveillance, so I readied a portable scrambling device in the bathroom to be sure I couldn't be recorded.

"About fifteen minutes later, I heard a knock at the door. When I answered it, to my relief, there was Marissa standing there with the big bastard I met by the skyway. He called her Mary, but I was certain that it was the girl in the picture. Poor thing looked worn out and sad despite the semblance of a smile she had on her face. I told him she was perfect and thanked him. She came into the room, sat on the bed, and began to undress herself. I stopped her and went into the bathroom to turn on my scrambler. When I came out of the bathroom, I asked her if her name was really Marissa. She nervously said it was.

"I smiled and said, 'We only have a few minutes before they check the cameras and audio equipment in the room. Alex sent me and he said to hold on because he's coming to get you.'

"I consoled her and told her to hurry and get herself together so that I could turn off my scrambler. I told her to make sure she was visible on the second floor tomorrow night so that we could get her out of here. She anxiously agreed. I went in the bathroom and told her to look as though she was putting her clothes back on. I turned my scrambler off and came out of the bathroom as though I was getting dressed again. I kissed her on the cheek and left the room. She's tired. We need to move her ASAP."

After Chuck told us what he saw, we finalized our plan to extract Marissa. We agreed that Michelle would distract Beaumont from keeping an eye on the girls who work the second floor. I would circulate around the second floor and locate Marissa while Walls had our backs, with Chuck and Glen watching us all to make sure no other spotters were looking out for working girls trying to flee. Once we had Marissa in a position where we could get her out, Glen would break away to get the car, and we would all leave and go to the airport. We were all a bit nervous about our plan and whether or not it would work, but it was what we had—and we knew we mustn't fail. I don't think any of us got much sleep that night.

CHAPTER 17

I woke up Friday morning with a sense of both excitement and dread: excited to be preparing to help someone in need but terrified by the prospect of failing. My concern was not for myself. If we failed, my friends could be hurt or killed, and an enslaved woman could be forced to continue a life of unimaginable horror.

I got up early and went for a run on the beach to take in the sunrise and the clear morning air. While jogging, I couldn't help but look over the horizon, knowing I would soon be heading into a situation that could go south very quickly. My mood was somber when I went to visit my parents that morning, but I played it off just enough to not let them know that something was up. Before heading to the airport, I made sure I saw my nieces and nephews, my cousins, and my sister, just in case things didn't go as planned. The four of us met at Edward's house to pick up some more cash in the event that something unanticipated arose and to let him know to be on standby in case we needed him. Edward also made sure that each of us had a Glock 19 in case things got a little dicey. We drove separately to the airport and met near Hangar 3.

It was about 9:30 p.m. when we took off. We exchanged few words as we all boarded the Piaggio Avanti Evo.

Once seated, I looked back at everyone onboard and said, "Last chance to say no."

They all looked at each other for a moment before Glen said, "We're with you, man. Let's go."

We taxied before being cleared and took off. The flight was smooth without many clouds in the sky, but as we started to make our descent, the reality of the situation began to set in. Everyone settled their anxiety and focused on what we needed to do.

We landed and briefly went over our assignments one last time before we jumped into the rented Escalade and headed to The Blue Trance. When we arrived, we parked around the corner from the club and entered separately. Chuck was already inside, waiting at a table near the bar, subtly motioning us where to station ourselves as he saw us enter the club. Michelle entered first to take Beaumont's attention away from the door and the activity on the floor. He was like putty in her hands from the moment he laid eyes on her. Glen stayed in a location near the door so he could keep an eye on us but to be in a position to get the car once we secured Marissa. Walls shadowed Michelle and Beaumont as he mingled with the crowd while I kept an eye out for Marissa.

About an hour passed without any sight of her. I could see Michelle was getting weary with entertaining someone as lame as Sam Beaumont. She soldiered on and kept him on a hook. Finally, after another ten minutes or so, I received a text from Chuck saying, "On your six!" I turned around and saw Marissa walking up the stairs followed by one of the goons charged with watching the working girls in the club. I fixated on Marissa so hard I almost didn't notice the familiar face on the woman walking next to her with the same wearied look as Marissa. Ifama, the nanny for my first passengers to the Tranquil Islands, was also being ushered upstairs along with Marissa. Chuck had told Marissa to look out for us when he saw her yesterday, so her head was on a swivel when she reached the top of the staircase. I sent a group text to everyone with me saying, "Look alive! I see her. By the staircase." That signaled Michelle to ditch Beaumont, Walls to follow Michelle to the exit, Glen to get the car, and Chuck to keep watch while moving closer to the door. Marissa caught eyes with me as I was making my way toward her and Ifama through the crowd. She slowed her pace so that our paths were sure to cross.

"Wow! You two have to be the sexiest women in the club. Is tonight my lucky night?" I said as I bumped into Marissa and Ifama. "These girls have a date already," said the goon ushering them toward the elevator.

"I didn't hear them say that."

"It's not for them to say," he replied.

"Oh… I see. It's like that. Okay. How much?"

"Three thousand dollars a girl, but they're already spoken for tonight."

Marissa and Ifama began to look anxious, so I had to come up with something fast before their eagerness began to make it obvious that something was in the works.

"I'll tell you what. How about $3,000 a girl and $1,500 for you being such a good businessman?"

He stood for a second and considered my proposal before saying, "Make it $3,000 for me, and you have a deal."

"Two thousand dollars for you," I said to not appear too easy.

He grinned and said, "I can live with that."

I reached into my sport coat pocket and peeled off $8,000 of the $10,000 that Edward gave me for walkaround money on the island. I put my arms around both ladies and began to walk toward the bar. I told the ladies to keep cool as we ordered drinks and sat next to Chuck to wait for Glen to return with the car. Michelle and Walls waited near the exit for Glen to bring the car up. About ten minutes later, Glen texted everyone that he was out front. We waited until the goon I paid the $8,000 to was not paying attention then made our way toward the door.

Everything was running smoothly until Beaumont came wandering up the stairs like a lost puppy, looking for Michelle. I could see him scanning the mezzanine for her as I neared the exit with Marissa and Ifama. We hurried out the door and rushed Marissa and Ifama down the steps and into the Escalade. As I began to climb in so that we could go to the airport, I felt someone grab my shoulder and spin me around. Before I got completely turned around, I could see a punch coming toward the center of my face. I slipped the punch and circled to face the attacker. I got my bearings and saw Beaumont squaring up to throw another punch. Before he could swing, I delivered a front kick to his solar plexus followed by an elbow to the temple, and he went down like a lead weight. By this time, the goon I had paid rushed me from the side and slammed me into the Escalade. Glen and Walls jumped out to engage the other two goons who had begun making their way down the steps of The Blue Trance. After slamming me into the car, my attacker attempted to lift me and throw me to the sidewalk. His only mistake was he grabbed me around my arms and torso versus my waist. This allowed me to lower my center of gravity and escape his hold by forcefully raising my arms laterally. Once free, I grabbed the back of his head in a Muay Thai clinch and delivered a series of knees to his ribs. I heard him wince loudly and felt something crack in his side on the third knee. He slowly dropped to his knees while clutching his side. I looked over and saw Glen take a right cross that sent him down to one knee. The goon who hit him went to follow that punch with a knee to Glen's face. With two hands close together, Glen blocked the knee and then shoulder-tackled the guy from one knee and slammed him onto the steps of The Blue Trance. I knew the guy was immediately unconscious from the way his head bounced off of the steps. Walls's guy was swinging for the fences and hitting nothing but air. On about the fifth swing, Walls ducked under the swing, delivered a short right hook to the guy's ribs, and followed it with a right cross to the guy's left temple, sending him stumbling back into a crowd of onlookers.

Walls began to press towards the guy to finish him off when Chuck jumped out of the Escalade and yelled, "Patrick get in the truck, son! We don't have time for that. We gotta go *now*! More are coming!"

We looked up and saw what looked like five more guys pushing their way through the crowd that had gathered. Walls broke free and made it into the truck. Glen jumped back in the driver's seat as Chuck and I jumped in, and we took off toward the airport. We sped through the city streets as fast as we could and finally got onto the road that led to the airport.

About a mile or so down that road, Chuck said, "We may not be out of the woods yet, boys and girls."

A set of headlights appeared in the rearview window, approaching fast, followed by another set of headlights. We began to hear the sounds of bullets whizzing past the vehicle. The rear windshield suddenly shattered!

"Get 'em off my ass!" Glen shouted. Michelle, Walls, Chuck, and I already had our pistols out as Glen was shouting. We rolled down our windows and began firing back as Marissa and Ifama did their best to lay low while screaming in fear. As we fired back, we noticed the first car take a sharp jerk to the right before overcorrecting and running into the path of the second car. The second car hit the first, allowing us to continue on to the airport unhindered.

"Anyone hit?" I asked.

After checking for several moments, everyone said a collective no as we continued down the road. We pulled directly up to the hangar where we left the plane.

As we were rushing toward the plane, Michelle said, "Arch! You're bleeding!"

What I didn't tell everyone was that a round grazed my shoulder when the rear windshield shattered. It was just a flesh wound, so I didn't say anything so we could stay focused on protecting ourselves and getting off the island. Everyone quickly boarded the plane as I fired up the engines. I didn't wait to be cleared to take off. I just taxied and took off down the nearest open runway. I pushed that Avanti so we could get back to Patrician as quickly as possible. Marissa and Ifama spent the hour-long flight holding one another's hands, clearly shaken up, and processing everything that was happening.

We touched down and quickly headed to Hangar 3 so we could get Marissa and Ifama into police protection. Once everyone deplaned, we quickly headed to the cars that were parked inside the hangar. I thought everything was good and this ordeal was over until I got to my Mustang and saw the lights turn on over the spot where our cars were parked. I turned around and saw the devil himself, James Parker, walk out of the shadows with a 9 mm pointed at us.

"I must say, Alex, I am both impressed and disappointed in you," he said as he walked toward us.

Michelle slowly began to move her hand toward her gun, thinking he wasn't watching.

He pointed his gun at her and said, "Don't do it, honey. I'll blow your pretty little face off your fucking skull." He turned back toward me and said, "You've kept the Mustang up well. I never expected to see that piece of shit riding around town again." He looked at all of us, took a deep breath, and said, "I'm impressed you got these two back to Florida. Took a lot of balls, man, but I'm disappointed. Disappointed that you had to have a fucking conscience."

He rubbed his head in a sort of frustrated confusion and continued to rant, "You think that I was paying you well, flying people to and from? Imagine how much I could have paid you to fly these bitches in for me? You almost ruined something that's really good for me. Thank goodness one of the security people at The Blue Trance called me when they saw you rushing these two broads out of the club. I own it, you know. Perfect place to keep the broads once I get 'em in. You could have had it even better than you had it, Alex, but now it's gotta come to an end for you. Goodbye, Alex."

Pow! Silence… I closed my eyes, bracing for the pain of a 9 mm slug impact. I was expecting to then hear a hail of gunfire as my crew returned fire, but the only sound I heard was the sound of a body hitting the ground. I opened my eyes to see James laying on the ground with blood spouting from a gunshot wound to his left temple.

"Damn! Took you long enough! I thought I was about to get shot," I said as Edward stepped in, holding a 9 mm pistol of his own.

"What the hell?" Glen said in shock.

"I thought you were just the money behind all of this," Michelle said in confusion.

"I was at first, until Alex and I went over a few logistics with Chuck."

"Yeah. I knew we'd need someone here to watch our backs at the airport. All the guys I know back in Spokane were tied up, so the only other person available was Mr. Moneybags here," Chuck said. "It took me a minute to get up the guts to agree, but after thinking about it, this was my wrong to right, and the burden of this should fall on my shoulders, not you all's."

"So how'd you get past the guard at the airport gate without being seen?"

"That was easy. Julia is always running food up to the hangars for the pilots, so I talked her into letting me hide in her trunk while she came up to put food in fridges for us. Didn't take much convincing once she knew what James was doing." He walked over to James's body and stood over him. After a moment, he continued, "I have a PI friend in Jacksonville that owed me a favor, so he drove down and tailed James so I could know when he was heading to the airport. Now you guys need to get yourselves and these girls out of here so I can get this cleaned up."

He turned to Chuck and asked, "You sure this scrambling thing is still scrambling the cameras in the hangar?"

"Stop worrying, Moneybags, and get this mess cleaned up. You're fine. The guards have likely been here to check it out a time or two while you were hiding in Hangar 4 and think the cameras are just acting up. It's after midnight and way past Ol' Chuck's bedtime. We'll see you tomorrow."

We all got into our vehicles and left the airport. Chuck headed back to his hotel room while the rest of us all stayed in a suite at the Ocean Harbor Hotel. Marissa and Ifama shed tears of joy and relief as they cried themselves to sleep. While we slept, Julia returned to Hangar 3 with her trunk lined with plastic. She and Edward loaded James's body in her trunk, cleaned up the blood, and left the airport with Edward hiding on the floor in the back seat. Once clear of the airport, Edward got into the passenger seat. When they got to the guard shack at his housing development, he pretended to be too intoxicated to drive home so Julia could look like the good designated-driver friend who got him home safely. Once at his home, they took James's body to Edward's dock where they loaded him onto his boat. Edward took the boat out several miles into the gulf and dumped James's body overboard with cinder blocks tied to it; this was fitting in his mind for a man whose actions led to his son meeting the same dismal end.

The next morning, Glen called Lt. Bradford and reported what he knew of Beaumont's actions. Turns out Bradford had begun to suspect Beaumont was involved because of what he was finding out in his investigation. Beaumont wasn't due back to work until Monday. His normal MO was to fly back to Patrician on Sunday and rest up before going to work the next day. Lt. Bradford and several officers were waiting. They arrested his sorry ass as he got off the plane.

CHAPTER 18

About a month passed before things appeared to return to a semblance of normalcy. James Parker was declared a missing person. Jack may have been kept separate from James's affairs, but that didn't mean he didn't know that his brother was into something. He put up a handsome reward for information about his brother's disappearance, but inside he had come to an understanding that his brother was likely dead because of his dealings. The nine of us who knew the truth about what happened to James swore to never tell anyone. As far as we were concerned, it was the price he paid for taking the freedom and, sadly in some cases, the lives away from women who wanted nothing more than to better themselves.

Matt finally awakened from his coma and, along with Marissa and Shawn Grundy, would later testify against Sam Beaumont in court. Beaumont and several other police officers were convicted and sentenced to life in prison for human trafficking and attempted murder. We later learned that Ifama's full name was Ifama Agwuegbo and that she was brought over to the United States from Lagos, Nigeria, by Ken and Marjorie Wellington. They were part of a human trafficking scheme involving doctors going to different countries in Africa and promising young women an opportunity to study medicine in America. They would stage some sort of competition; African women would be typically challenged to write an essay or make a video, detailing why they should be chosen for this phony program. Once they were selected, the women were brought over to live in what they thought was a host home until it was time for them to begin medical school. Instead, the women were either forced to work without compensation for the person who brought them over or sold to someone else. In Ifama's case, she was made to work for the Wellingtons who later sold her to James Parker. Parker made her, Marissa, and countless other women give their bodies to men for sex so he could make money. For their part in the scam, they were both sentenced to life in prison as well.

For some reason, I thought that after getting the young ladies to safety, we would sort of ride off into the proverbial sunset and return to our everyday lives. In my mind, everyone would go on like normal, but that's not exactly what happened. Chuck and Walls returned home to Washington, but after all the excitement, Walls decided he would transfer down to MacDill AFB when the opportunity presented itself. Chuck stayed in contact with us and even bought himself a vacation home in Patrician. In classic Chuck fashion, he pops into town without us even knowing. Glen and I will sometimes go to pay for our drinks when we're hanging out at The Dunes with Robert and Allen, only to have the waitress say, "The gentleman in the back took care of you guys," as we look to the back of the restaurant and see Chuck raising his glass to us.

Michelle got bored with sitting at home and doing nothing, so I helped her get a job flying with me at Patrician Gulf. She loves the money and the opportunity to team up with Devin and talk noise to me.

I look in on Edward as much as I can. In his mind, he had set things right for Jeff and Rebecca being killed, but taking the life of another human being didn't sit too well with him at first. He finally took comfort in knowing that his actions helped to stop more Rebeccas, Marissas, and Ifamas from becoming sex slaves from Patrician.

After his disappearance, more information began to surface on the streets about James Parker. He had been providing escorts for many of the city's dignitaries. Everyone from doctors, lawyers, judges, and politicians were in James's back pocket because of what he knew about them. His disappearance set a lot of people at ease in a morbid sort of way.

Instead of returning to Connecticut and Nigeria respectively, Marissa and Ifama stayed in Patrician. They told us that they both arrived on St. Cesare's Island around the same time and bonded immediately. A sisterhood formed between them during their ordeal, and they promised to support one another while in their captivity. Michelle had extra space at her new home, so she opened her doors to them for as long as they needed. Shortly after, they moved into one of Matt's condos on the beach. Having a near-death experience gave Matt a new lease on life, even more than almost losing his life, knowing he played a part in helping to positively change the lives of two people really affected his outlook on life.

He was still very much focused on his business and making money, but now he understood that helping people was more rewarding than any deal he'd ever close. He'll never admit it, but I know he refused to charge Marissa and Ifama for the condo. He moved them in right next to the one that he gave to his parents, and from what they say, he looks out for them and makes sure they're okay. Robert got them both jobs as tellers at the bank. Rayna had quickly moved into being the lead financial analyst at the bank. She was still playing hard to get with me, but she promised me that she would look after them. With Rayna training them, it wasn't long before they moved into being new accounts managers. They were very proud of their promotions, but more than that, they were proud of what they began to accomplish in the community.

About three months after they began working at the bank, Marissa and Ifama started a nonprofit organization designed to educate women how to recognize the signs of human trafficking in their communities. They began traveling and sharing their story all over the country to tell people how easily a person can be trafficked if they, or people around them, are not paying attention.

One Sunday in the latter part of spring, Reverend Johnson invited Marissa and Ifama to share their story with the congregation. After they accepted, Reverend Johnson reached out to several churches and community leaders around Patrician to spread the word about the service, resulting in a very large turnout that Sunday morning. Both Marissa and Ifama insisted that Glen and I and everyone involved, be there to hear them speak. None of us wanted to be acknowledged for our actions. At the end of the day, we just did what we felt people should do when they see others in need. We just wanted them to have their time and wanted them to be recognized for their resilience and their decision to never give up. Glen, Michelle, and I met at my parents' house and walked over to the church. Not long after we sat down, Walls and Chuck entered the church, followed by Edward, his wife, and Julia. Matt and his parents sat a row behind us, as did Shawn Grundy, his wife, his daughters, and his sister, Tasha. Before the service, Marissa asked me to step aside so that she could talk to me. As she usually does, she gave me a big hug and started telling me what was on her mind.

"I've thanked you a million times for rescuing me. You never gave up on me even when I found myself in trouble a second time. I've never thanked you for helping restore my faith, though."

"Your faith?"

"Yeah, my faith. Some people don't believe in God, and that's their prerogative, but I was always taught to. Daddy may have been into some bad things before he was killed, but he always made sure that I went to church. He wouldn't set foot inside of one. He had a joke that he would probably catch fire if he walked inside of one, but he'd always walk me to Sunday school and pick me up when I was a little girl. Anyway, when I was taken the first time, it was tough, of course, but I kept believing that God wouldn't let me go through this. The second time, though, I started to doubt. I prayed and prayed that I would get out of that situation but it got worse. One night, one really…bad… night on the island, I began to feel that I had no reason to live anymore. I saw no way out. I cried and cried that entire night. In the middle of one of my crying sessions, I said, 'God, if you're listening, please help me get out of here. If you do, I'll live a good life!' Nothing happened. Nothing happened for what seemed like forever. I finally gave up. I resigned to the fact that I would be a sex slave until I die or they kill me."

She paused, wiped her eyes, got her composure, looked me in the eyes, and said, "But then I heard you say my name that night when I got on the elevator. The look you had on your face said, 'Hold on, Marissa! Just hold on!' It was at that moment that I knew God heard me when I asked him to help me. So thank you, big bro, for not just rescuing me but for letting me know that God did hear me. You are a real answer to my prayers, and I'm going to live a good life!"

Now, I am not an emotional man, but I had a few tears trickling down my face by this time. Just as I wiped them away, Ifama was walking up with an usher so she and Marissa could take the stage and share their story. I went back to my seat once I dried my eyes. The crowd sat there stunned as Marissa and Ifama detailed their ordeal. There are no words to explain how proud I was of these two young ladies. By looking at them, you couldn't tell that these two women were only a few months removed from the most horrific time of their lives. As they began to wind down their time on stage, they encouraged everyone to be vigilant and willing to help a person in need. Marissa concluded the message by saying, "If you see something suspicious, say something and do something about it." I thought to myself, *Thank God I did.*

THE END

ABOUT THE AUTHOR

To put it plainly, Brian Simpson grew up all over the United States. By the time he was sixteen, his father's career in the Marine Corps took him from his birthplace of New Smyrna Beach, Florida, to North Carolina, California, and Virginia. During this time, Brian developed a love for travel, writing, sports, music, and aviation. He has been an educator and coach at both the high school and college levels as well as held a career in sales and marketing. A self-professed movie buff and "pizza snob," Brian enjoys spending time with family and friends.